the GAME

the GAME

Teresa Toten

Red Deer PRESS

The Publishers
Red Deer Press
813 MacKimmie Library Tower
2500 University Drive N.W.
Calgary Alberta Canada T2N 1N4
www.reddeerpress.com

Credits
Edited for the Press by Peter Carver
Cover and text design by Duncan Campbell
Cover photograph courtesy of Robert Karpa/Masterfile
Printed and bound in Canada by Friesens for Red Deer Press

Acknowledgments
Financial support provided by the Canada Council, the Department of Canadian Heritage, the Alberta Foundation for the Arts, a beneficiary of the Lottery Fund of the Government of Alberta, and the University of Calgary.

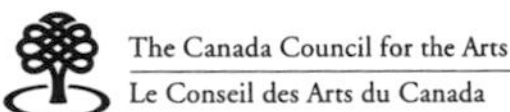

National Library of Canada Cataloguing in Publication Data

Toten, Teresa, 1955–
The game

ISBN 0-88995-232-9

I. Title.
PS8589.06759G35 2001 C813'.54 C2001-910210-0
PR9199.3.T6165G35 2001

5 4 3 2 1

Author's Acknowledgments

This book has struggled for five years to find its feet. If it stands now it is only because of my husband, who believed before there was anything to believe in; my writing group: Susan Adach, Ann Goldring, Nancy Hartry, and Loris Lesynski, breathtaking writers all; Dr. Nadira Lakdawalla; all those patient "ears" in Bronxville, N.Y.; and my editor Peter Carver.

For Ken

For Always

As Lightning to the Children eased
With explanation kind
The Truth must dazzle gradually
Or every man be blind—

–Emily Dickinson

PROLOGUE

William Thurber ripped off his cummerbund and groaned with relief as he stuffed it into his tuxedo pocket. "Ah-h-h-h-h . . . damn, that's good." He also tried to loosen his bow tie, but he was too tired and only managed to knot it tighter. By the time he got to the isolation corridor, he was almost choking.

"Heya, Doc!" The supervising orderly greeted him with a solid thump on the back. "What the hell you doing here? It's midnight!" Without looking, Harold snapped the short end of the mangled tie, instantly setting it free. He held up his hand. "I know, I know, the missus used to do that stuff for ya. But ya still shouldn't be here, even if yas don't know how to undress yourself." Harold lumbered back to the computer station. "Look, everything's cool. Bobby Sullivan is out and back at C Ward as of last night and . . . what?"

Over the years, Thurber had almost grown accustomed to Harold's appearance—the arms writhing with tattoos, and the ears and even one eyebrow pierced with an increasing assortment of studs and rings. Almost. Without fail, it was the orderly's head that always caught him off guard. When it wasn't shaved, it was spiked or dyed or all three. Today's color was a spectacularly gruesome shade of fuscia.

"Like your hair," said Thurber. "Is that supposed to be pink?"

"Yeah, the kids are really into it," Harold beamed as he handed over the daily charts.

"Nice," nodded Thurber, flipping through the charts. "They called me on the Webster girl this morning."

"Aw-h-h-h . . . they shouldn't have oughtta done that," growled Harold. "She's been stable for over eight hours. The residents were on it. Besides, what was ya gonna do from Boston?"

"I asked them to call. I should've been here for the transfer from Westchester General instead of with those penguins at Harvard." Thurber squinted at the girl's chart. "Detox, seventy-two hours! Why wasn't I notified? Seventy-two hours!"

"Cool your jets, Doc." Harold reached for his arm. "Westchester did the assessment, and like I said, the residents were on her from the moment she got here. You didn't see her. The kid had a pharmacy running through her veins, not just the vodka."

"The mother says . . . she said . . . that that was recent." Thurber swallowed. "What was Westchester's assessment?"

"The pills, a few months," Harold shrugged. "The vodka . . . longer."

"More than a year?" Thurber massaged his temples.

"Probably," said Harold.

Thurber headed toward a small corridor behind the computer terminal. He tore open a curtain covering a large one-way window and glared into the blue room. A young girl with chopped up hair huddled on a bedsheet on the floor. He thought she was sleeping, then noticed one eye closed and the other wide open, staring at the door.

"Harold!"

"Now, don't get your knickers in a knot." Harold moved in closer to the window. "Her vitals are as good as it gets, but she's been nonresponsive for about four hours."

Danielle Webster looked as if she had been tossed into the corner like a discarded toy. It hurt to look. Thurber slammed his fist into the wall.

"Ow!"

"You're gonna bust open your hand one of these days, and then what?" Harold went back to the computer, muttering to himself. "It says here that sometimes she changes the eye thing, and then," he looked back up at the doctor, "about an hour ago she started to sing, kind of. . . ."

"Sing?" Thurber examined the girl, noting her color, rigidity, fixed gaze. Danielle Webster was frozen. "Sing what?"

"Beats me," shrugged Harold. "Nothing from Pearl Jam. Maybe a lullaby type of thing?"

"Get her off the floor and cover her up," said Thurber.

"We been doing that on every single check, Doc. Want her strapped in?"

"No," Thurber slumped. "No, she's not hurting herself."

"Come on," Harold tried to usher Thurber away, "she's being checked every half hour."

Thurber nodded.

"You're bagged, Doc. I'll call ya a cab."

"Yeah, I just want to . . ." Thurber trailed back to the Isolation window. Harold waited for a moment and then joined him. "Yes, Harold?"

"Yolanda left you two fresh pillows and a blanket in your coat closet. You know, the little room with the door where you're supposed to put your coat?"

"Thanks."

The girl curled up tighter and started to shiver. Was she cold? Was she scared? "Harold," Thurber leaned his forehead against the window, "call up a nurse and let's get this kid back up on her bed."

"You got it, Doc."

He didn't take his eyes off her. She seemed to be watching him just as intently.

But that wasn't possible.

"What the hell did they do to you?" he whispered.

As if in answer, the girl began to sing.

Isolation, F Ward, February 11, 8:36 p.m.

It was a small room, arid and empty. Except for the bed and, of course, the girl.

"No!" Dani flung her arms to her face. "No more! No, Daddy, Daddy please . . ." She bolted up gulping air as if it were water. Waiting and gulping.

"Oh . . . God, oh God, where . . ." Her heart careened around her chest. Her mouth felt stuffed with aluminum foil. But the worst was her hair. Every strand hurt.

"I'll just shut my eyes a sec." Immediately, her head took off and helicoptered around the room. She popped her eyes back open.

"Oops, guess not."

But having both eyes open was almost as bad. After some painful experiments, Dani compromised on closing her right eye and looking out with her left. That settled, she clutched the mattress and tried to sit up. It was so-o-o hot. Her T-shirt was plastered with sweat. Wait, this wasn't her shirt. How—Dani crooked her eyes and stretched out the front of the T-shirt: "RUN FOR MENTAL HEALTH THE RIVERWOOD NEEDS YOU!"

"The Riverwood?" She pressed back in against the headboard. "Oh, man, where am I?"

9:11 P.M.

Dani tried to focus on the room. Single bed, tubular frame, pillow, no pillowcase, faded blue sheet. Still peering through one open eye and clinging to the sheet for support, she hauled herself up. No nightstand, no lamp, no chest of drawers, nothing, just the bed. No windows, absolutely no windows, not even on the door. "Door? Door!" Dani lurched toward it, struggling with the sheet the whole way. When she finally got there, she fell and yanked at the same time.

"Hello, I'm awake now." She got up, yanked again.

"Out, please." Both eyes open. Yank.

"Please?" Dani's head started revving for takeoff. Sliding to the floor, she glued her right eye shut again.

"Anybody?"

9:35 P.M.

Sitting cross-legged on the floor, Dani began tenderly rearranging the blue sheet. "Course it's locked." Patting here. "It's always locked." Smoothing there. "The door is always locked in those books, locked in those movies. So it's going to have to be locked in my nightmare. Or else, why bother having a nightmare? Now, I ask me?"

She killed a giggle before it could turn on her.

Dani stroked the sheet and then the walls. "Blue walls. That's wrong, I think. Pink is what calms down lunatics . . . Restful Rose. Yeah. No. That's not it. Pink is for prisons. It calms down criminals. Blue must be for . . . Blissful Blue.

"Somebody . . . Somebody, come down. Or up, or, or, whatever . . . Please."

9:52 P.M.

The floor was nice. Inviting really, gleaming and burning cold.

No.

She was still burning, but the floor was cold. It was a polished stone with sparkly bits in it that were moving. Yup, teeny little diamond specks dancing brightly, making her head do laps around the room.

"I am not nuts. I *know* the floor shouldn't be moving. I don't want the floor to move. I'll be good. Make it stop."

She remembered the vodka then.

Bad.

All that vodka. And pills? How many pills?

Very, very bad.

"Sorry. Sorry. Hello, somebody! I'm sorry. I'm so sorry. Can I go now?"

Very, very, very bad.

10:10 P.M.

"Ignorant Little Cow!"

"Don't!" Dani swung her head, risking certain decapitation.

"Daddy?" There was no one, just the sound of her blood

swishing and chugging around inside of her. Breathing was tough. "Daddy?"

Nope. Just blue.

Their basement walls were blue, and the cops wore blue. No, they weren't cops, but the light was flashing. Dani winced, flushed with shame. "Whoa, God, it was an ambulance. Sorry. Sorry."

She stretched out her T-shirt and strained to reread the letters. "The . . . Riverwood? The . . . Oh God! The Riverwood Clinic? Holy . . . no, no, it can't . . . I wouldn't . . . couldn't." Fear rolled over her and shoved her into the door. "The Riverwood! Kelly, sh-h-h-h . . . hang on, sh-h-h-h . . . I'll just . . . be sh-h-h-h. I'll . . ."

10:31 P.M.

Had someone come in? No, how could they? Dani and her sheet were both puddled against the door. "Can't get in, can't get out."

She giggled.

It hurt.

But there was something . . . something knocking on the door.

"Hey! Are you in there or what?" the door said. "Danielle Webster?"

Dani shut both her eyes in order to hear the door better.

"Are you Danielle Irene Webster?"

"Can I go now?"

"Shut up and answer the question."

Bossy door. You can't shut up *and* answer a question.

"Are you Danielle Webster?"

Dani nodded.

"Are ya deaf?" the door shouted. "Are you Danielle Irene—"

"Oh. Yeah, yes!" said Dani. "That's me. Dani."

"Groovy. I'm Scratch. I think you're my new roomie."

She was going to be rooming with a door in this teeny little blue space? There was just the one bed. "Uh . . . where . . . ?"

"Not now, I can't stay here forever—they're checking you, like, every two minutes. I hacked into your Intake Admissions yesterday, and man, oh man."

People came? "Do they come in here? I haven't left the door, I mean, you, so—"

"Oh, brother. Like I said, they're sticking you with me and I just need to know, from you, not them . . . so . . . just how nuts are you?"

Dani didn't like the door. Rude, bossy door. "Nuts?" She stretched out her T-shirt top again. "I am not . . . I just, uh . . . too much vodka. Accidentally." Yes, that was it. That was definitely it. She caught sight of a memory and zeroed in on a flash of the emergency room in Westchester General. "Too much."

Or was that the time before?

"Yeah, right," sighed the door. "Well, let's not lose touch. Gotta go. Look, kid, uh, don't fight it or they'll nail you. I've read your charts. You're so full of benzodiazepines I'm surprised you can talk. I'll see you in about a day, and we can pretend to bond then. Stay loose."

Ben who?

And just where did the door think it was going?

"Hey!" Dani called. "Why am I here?" No answer. Stay loose? Dani was already so loose she couldn't get up. She had to figure out how to get unloose, stiffen up in fact.

"Hey! Come back! I'll stop doing it."

No answer.

"Whatever it was. I'll stop."

But the door wasn't listening.

11:01 P.M.

Dani finally saw the mirror. She refocused her right eye. "Perfect." The mirror was huge and suspended on the wall opposite her bed. "What's a good nightmare without a mirror?"

She slid up the wall, hugging the sheet for support. Halfway up, Dani was hit by a hurricane of nausea. "Okay. Okay. Everybody steady. One, two, three, let's breathe now, in then out. That's good, okay girls, we're going for the mirror."

Even fully stretched out, Dani's fingertips barely touched the mirror's edges. She couldn't really see her reflection. What kind of place was this with bossy doors and mirrorless mirrors? She embraced the mirror and placed one scalding cheek against it. Then the other. Then her forehead. Dani became mesmerized by the clouds created with her breath. She slowly raised her finger and started to draw clouds in the clouds.

"I know you're behind there. I've seen all the movies. You're taking notes and shaking your heads. This is illegal. Kidnapping a juvenile. I'm only fourteen or . . ." Her birthday was coming? Is coming? Went? ". . . or fifteen . . . My dad's a lawyer. . . . *Loser!*"

This time she knew not to look. He wasn't really there, and the floor wasn't really moving.

"Hello in there. I won't be bad anymore. Please. Okay?

Somebody come now or I'm going to have to wake up and ruin everything."

She squashed her face into the mirror. "Did the Ghost bring me here? Did she? Are you in there with the notetaker's mother?"

11:57 P.M.

A cramp and an image ripped through her at the same time. The combination yanked Dani to the floor. She tried to focus, working hard to excavate the memory.

It's a brilliant autumn day. They're at the old house near the ravine. A thousand little piles of leaves dot the rambling garden. Kelly toddles and tumbles into each and every mound, scattering everything. Dani and her mother are singing.

"Again, Mommy, again."

Mommy runs, swoops them both into her arms.

Lavender's blue, dilly dilly
lavender's green.
When I am king, dilly dilly
You shall be queen.
Who told you so, dilly dilly?

Who told you so?

Hot tears rushed to Dani's eyes and evaporated. The song faded, and the memory dissolved. Dani stared at her hands, searching for the misplaced pictures.

"Fine. . . . Back to bed."

She crawled, the sheet snaking around her hands and knees,

making her stumble. When she finally got close to the mattress, she knew there was no hope of actually getting up and onto it.

Dani spread out the sheet, trying to cover the whole troublesome floor. Stroking and smoothing the little folds, the tiny creases. She lay down.

"Somebody? Door? Could you come now, please? Couldn't somebody come? Just once, couldn't . . ."

'Twas my own heart, dilly dilly . . .

The cramps moved like lightning now, attacking different places, surprising her each time. She could never brace herself for the next one.

Just as she began gulping air again, an aroma came out of nowhere and covered her. It was the smell of their old kitchen and breakfasts from when they were little. But the smell was different from her father's voice, or the song.

The smell was real.

It had been so long. But it was real. It was here. The room waved under the power of crushed cinnamon. Everything charged with its pure, perfect scent.

"Okay, Kelly, I'm coming." Okay. It would be okay after all. There was still the Game. It would all be okay. Dani braced herself, shut both eyes and . . . followed.

. . . that told me so.

Twenty-One Months Ago

It was sunny that last time. Not that it mattered. For years, Dani and Kelly had taken off in all kinds of weather, including rain and howling winds. They just incorporated the elements into the Game. The weather would become a portent of how the battle would go that day. Sunny was good, though. Sunny was always good.

The two girls raced like always on their bikes, and like always Dani won—but just barely. Kelly was getting bigger and stronger by the minute. It was already difficult to tell which was the big sister. They ditched their bikes at the corner mailbox and snuck over to the side of old man Allen's house. His backyard butted the ravine slope—the entrance—perfectly. Old man Allen hated kids generally and the Webster girls specifically. He swore up and down that if he caught them skulking around his property, "just one more godamned time," he'd call the cops. "No warning, you little turds!"

That just made the whole thing tastier.

Kelly swung hard around and onto the path leading to old man Allen's backyard, almost knocking over her sister.

"Ow!" Dani nudged her sister back into the rolled up garden hose. "You are such an oaf!"

"It's part of my charm," said Kelly, clutching her stomach.

"Didn't you go pee before we left, for Godsake?" asked Dani. "I told you to go pee." This, too, was part of Kelly's charm. It seemed to Dani that Kelly always had to go but never actually went.

"Sure," she said, dancing from one foot to the other. "I went."

"Okay, so quit bopping around." Dani sighed and stretched against the warm bricks of the house. She shoved her shoulder blades against the rough brick until she could feel each ridge. "It is a powerful day for magic, Kelly. Do you sense the current? Do you hear the Game calling us?"

"You bet, uh-huh," said Kelly.

Dani smiled and splayed her body against the bricks in a star shape. "Okay . . . mark me, young warrior. Are you ready to go where no prepubescent has gone before?"

"For sure, yup, let's go." Kelly crouched into starting position. "What's prepuppy essence?"

"Prepubescence, young warrior. It means before teenager-hood."

"Oh yeah, I knew that. I just forgot."

Dani inhaled deeply, dramatically. "Yes, the magic will run very high today indeed."

"Yup. So are we going or what? Huh?"

"Ready?"

"All ready."

"Steady?"

"All steady."

They aimed for a wall of ancient lilac trees that edged the top of the ravine. The lilacs were at the very end of old man Allen's enormous weed-infested lawn. It felt a million miles away.

"Go!"

"Yes!"

It just didn't get better than that run toward the Game. Those exact seconds, right then . . . across the green.

The world inhaled.

They were lightning bolts across the lawn. Nearing the edge, they dove commando-style over the weeds and into the lilacs. Dani usually protected her face but landed hard on her stomach. Kelly always broke her landing but ate twigs going in.

"Good to be back, huh?" Kelly spit out a leaf.

"Perfect," Dani heaved. "My stomach is still in my mouth, but yeah, it's pretty perfect."

Kelly inched over to the top of the slope. She hung her head and shoulders over the embankment and stared down.

"Uh, I been thinking." Her arms dangled in the air over her head. "So the thing I was thinking was that I was, well . . . we should just . . . uh, stay or something . . . you know? Dani? Okay?"

Dani stopped breathing.

Kelly hauled herself up but didn't look at her sister. She kept looking into the ravine.

"I know it's worse. For you, I mean, and . . . don't think . . . I mean, I know it is."

The smell of the lilacs started to weigh on Dani like poured concrete.

"He's . . . I mean, it's like he's gearing up again. I know stuff.

It doesn't matter how much you don't want me to know. I'm not stupid, I know . . . your ear was, you know . . ."

The smell was so thick and syrupy that Dani could hardly breathe. Lilacs were her favorite flower. Lilacs. And now she couldn't breathe. What else? Betrayed by lilacs. What else did she have to do? Where else was there to go? The lilacs were hurting, for Godsake!

"Shut up, Kelly!"

"I just . . ."

"I said shut up and I mean shut up!"

Kelly looked like she'd been slapped.

Dani wanted to slap herself.

"Darn, Kelly, sorry, sorry. But we decided, we agreed, like, a hundred bazillion times already. We don't bring them here. Especially not him. Never. Here is only for us. The Game is only for us. Okay? We agreed, didn't we, huh?"

Her sister looked . . . what? . . . frightened?

"Just for us, remember? Our quest. I made, I mean, we made it, for us. There is no room for them here, what with all our creatures and beasts. We must never lose our focus." She reached over and touched Kelly's cheek. "Even though we quest to set the Goddess free, our primary burden is still to destroy the evil, to vanquish Yuras." She lowered her voice. "A mere mention of our parents could corrupt this quest. They are not welcome here, young warrior."

"Don't give me that." Kelly edged back over to Dani and stuck her face into hers, freckles to freckles. "You didn't even want to come." Dani started to protest, but Kelly placed muddy fingers over her sister's mouth. "I know you didn't." Nose pressed to nose. "You're faking it, but I don't care. At least we're here. And it'll come back to you. It always does. The magic is still strong." Kelly nodded fiercely. "It'll hold." She looked back down into the ravine. "Did you bring it?"

"Of course." Dani patted her pocket. "It is time." She tried to breathe through lilacs and look dignified while dragging her stomach over to the ridge. Kelly lined up beside her. "It is an especially fine day for magic, isn't it, young warrior?"

Kelly's eyes caught fire, gold on gold. "I sense it, Dani. Really I do."

"Ready?"

They were electric then, that day, as one charge, one child, one life.

"All ready."

"Steady?"

Dani could feel Kelly's heart beating.

"Steady."

"Now!"

Dr. William Thurber February 13
Clinical Director
Riverwood Youth Clinic
Riverwood, New York
10621

Dear Dr. Thurber,

I would like to apologize for my tone during our last telephone conversation. I continue to appall myself. Clearly, hospitalizing Dani was a trauma. I must have known that sifting through all the photos you requested would be another one. Nevertheless, I am enclosing the photo album which features her most prominently. They're lovely photos, really. Mark was, is, meticulous about that sort of thing. Understandably, there aren't any from the past year or so.

I believe our family physician has faxed Dani's pediatric records to Admissions. Admissions also has my new address and all the new phone numbers. Please don't direct any wrath on to poor old Dr. Slavin. It would be misguided. He's a gentle soul who didn't stand a chance against Mark. We were all so well trained and in the end, each injury was explainable.

Once I started looking at the photographs I couldn't stop, of course. I hated to let the photographs go, to let Dani go. What if I get neither back? Wait until you see. She was such a beautiful baby. She looks so very much like my father. The devil of black Irish as my mother would say.

My husband despises my father.

I remember the nurses at Mount Sinai lined up to bathe and coddle her. She really was that delicious. That someone like me . . . well, if I could have breathed for her I would have. He must have begun hating her even before we left the hospital.

What haunts me even more are the pictures of Dani and Kelly together. Look hard at those photos. Make Dani look, make her see. Look at how a three-year-old cradles and comforts her baby sister. Look at all of us during those family outings. It's Dani's hand that's firmly gripping Kelly's, Dani's thin little arms thrown protectively over Kelly's. What is crystal clear from every single picture is that Dani protected Kelly like a tigress. If you could just make her see.

Thank you for your updates and for your support. I've followed your suggestion and set up bi-weekly meetings with Dr. Richardson. I plan to look forward to each and every one of them by telling myself that this is the beginning, not the end. Isn't it?

Sincerely,
Sandra Webster

February 15, 8:00 a.m.

It seemed as if Dani had spent her entire life in the little blue room. It got so she couldn't remember anything else. Yet as soon as a nurse came and took her to something called the infirmary, Dani wondered whether the blue room had existed at all. Actually, Dani just assumed that the lady was a nurse because she had that nurse-thingy in her tone of voice. The way that all teachers have that teacher-thingy happening. No one here wore those puke green outfits that were standard issue at Westchester General. A couple of people sported stethoscopes that they were forever sticking on her chest and back, but that was about it. It was kind of sneaky. How was she supposed to know who to be nice to?

Dani was showered, shampooed, fed, and given two complete physicals. Blood was taken, injections given, and pills swallowed. Everything that could be peed in, monitored, and measured was. The stethoscopes asked lots of questions. The same questions. Dani wanted to be nice—to "cooperate"—but she kept forgetting what the questions were before she could answer any of them. Then the stethoscopes would drone on about her medication program over the coming weeks.

Weeks?

It was all "zine" this and "zine" that when it came to the drugs, mixed in with dollops of weasel words like "self-care" and "healing." The only thing Dani could consistently remember to remember was that she was in trouble. Big trouble.

By the time she changed into fresh clothes, Dani felt like she had spent her entire life in the infirmary. After lunch, a mountain of a nurse came in and took her vitals. Someone was always taking her "vitals." Apparently, her vitals were vital. Dani stared at the woman's erupting chest, straining to make out the letters on her name tag. "Yolanda L. Briggs." She seemed vaguely familiar, not her voice or her size, but . . . something.

"Okay, Dani girl. Time to meet your new world."

Dani fused herself to the table and forgot to breathe. Her fingers blurred, then disappeared into the white paper sheet covering the examining table. *Safe, not safe, safe, not safe.*

"Listen to me, girl." Yolanda fussed with Dani's T-shirt and ran her hands through Dani's stubby hair. "It has all started. You are getting better already. I know these things. Ask anybody. Now, darling, see those baby doctors?" She pointed to two stethoscopes in jeans. "They're residents, and they're watching your every twitch while pretending not to. So, my little angel, do yourself a favor and get off your butt!"

Dani popped off the table.

Yolanda swayed down painfully bright corridors with Dani trailing miserably. Dani staggered under the familiar stench of Benjamin Moore semigloss.

Yolanda turned back to her frowning. "It's just paint, darling. We've been renovating these old bones nonstop from the moment we opened the doors seven years ago. You'll get used to it."

"Yeah," nodded Dani. It's home away from home all right. Dani expected her mother to materialize under one of the ladders, brandishing fabric swatches. The place was a maze. They went up stairs and down sloping hallways. They glided through glass doors that whizzed open as soon as they saw you coming. *Whssst . . .* they'd open; *whssst . . .* they'd close. Glancing outside the windows whenever she could, Dani figured she was in some kind of national park. Kelly would love the whole thing. All it needed was a moat. Finally, they got on an elevator and went up—or was it down?—to a soft green corridor. Yolanda Briggs stopped at door 322 and pounded on it with an open hand. Dani was still puzzling over the open hand when the door opened. A fastidious-looking blonde took them both in while neatly arranging her face into a welcoming smile.

"Hey, Yo. What's up?" The smile broadened.

Dani recognized the voice and fell into the doorframe. There were too many things to take in, to keep track of.

"As if you didn't know," snorted Yolanda. "Danielle, Dani Webster, I would like to introduce you to your new roommate, Alison Hilary Mackenzie."

"That's Scratch to you."

Yup, it was the voice, the same voice. It wasn't so much that the girl looked fastidious as she smelled fastidious. Dani's roommate wreaked of lemon-scented Clorox. She wore an extra-large GAP sweatsuit with a white turtleneck underneath. Clearly the sweatsuit had been ironed. Who would iron sweats, for Godsake? What was the thinking here?

Dani wanted to bolt.

Instead, Yolanda guided her into the room. "It will never be Scratch to me, darling. This is your new home, honey." She welcomed Dani in with a small and perfect gesture.

Dani didn't move. Should she smile? At whom?

"God, Yo, does it talk?"

Yolanda sighed heavily. She rolled her head over to a door on their left. "This, dear child, is your private bathroom, except that it isn't private. For your own dignity, remember that. You're to keep in mind that there is no lock on that door and staff can and will, at any moment, barge in." Did she look embarrassed? "I know it's an ugly thought, dear girl, but it's uglier if we don't. So now you know." She strolled over to the far bed and patted the paisley- patterned quilt. "Take a load off, little one. Your things won't get here until this evening."

Dani shuffled over and sat on the very outermost edge of the quilt.

"Fabulous," said Scratch. "I can just tell we're going to be the best of friends. We'll share secrets, exchange recipes . . ."

"Like you were Miss Congeniality when we first poured you in here," snorted the nurse. She turned to the dresser, the top of which displayed a collection of nail polishes that would have been the envy of any drugstore. Dani noticed that her new roommate was clenching her jaw and smiling at the same time. Dani knew this particular combination. She could spot it a mile away. After catching Alison's eye, Yolanda began to rearrange the already perfectly arranged bottles of nail polish.

"Hey, Yo. You want to tell our little fawn here what the 'L' in Yolanda L. Briggs stands for?"

Yolanda didn't even glance up. "Now, honey, I don't know why you don't believe me. I keep telling you the 'L' stands for 'Luscious.'" She smiled broadly at a clear nail polish bottle.

Dani didn't know where to look. The nail polish thing seemed to be some kind of private code or test. Every so often, Yolanda would glance back at Alison, who just kept up with that smile thing.

"Well," said Yolanda, finally satisfied with her alignment of darkest to lightest shades. "Now, I'm going to leave you two to curl your hair and discuss Leonardo Di Caprio or whatever itty-bitty white chicks do at a sleepover." She placed a yellow sheet of paper in Dani's hand. "This, darling, is your life for the next three days. After that, you get a different sheet for every single day telling you where to go, when to eat, and when to fart. We don't want you to bother with that kind of teeny tiny thinking. You got to be thinking just big thoughts about how to get out of this place, right?" She was raising and lowering her eyebrows at Dani.

Dani was mesmerized. How could she not have noticed those eyebrows before? They were tidy little things, straight and friendly, but extremely bushy. They looked like agitated caterpillars.

"You just go to your French class, one-on-one, Little Group . . . whatever it says there," she tapped on the paper, "and get your bony butt to whatever it says, when it says." She turned and swayed out of the room. "I'm watching you, Alison. You're ready, girl."

"Whoa!" Scratch shot over to Yolanda. "You stick me with a stomach pumper and you're watching *me?*"

Yolanda didn't even break stride. "That's right, Alison dear."

"That's Scratch to you," she muttered. As soon as the door was shut, Scratch slipped over to the dresser and with shaking hands she realigned each bottle from largest to smallest. With that task completed she seemed relieved enough to turn her attention back to Dani. "Let's see." She grabbed Dani's yellow sheet. "One-on-one . . . with Thurber right off the bat, hmmmm. They gave you the Grand Pooh Bah. I mean, Dr. Richardson is bearable and everything, but Thurber . . . you must be really nuts or really loaded." Scratch re-examined her nail polish rows.

Dani felt like she had just fallen into the rabbit hole. Was this an institution for the compulsively neat?

"Thurber likes to start off with the photo albums. You got to play along. . . . It's his thing. He's, like, famous for it. You go for the photos, and you're on your way out. Got it?"

Dani stared back at Scratch with increasing confusion.

"Anyway," shrugged Scratch, "it's all touchy-feely. Find a photo and go for it, make it up, whatever it takes. You got to show them willingness or . . . what the hell are you staring at?"

"Are you the door?" asked Dani

"Oh fart," groaned Scratch. She snapped her fingers in front of Dani's face.

Daddy did that.

"Look, space cadet."

Scratch seemed to be angry with her. Maybe Dani wasn't being nice enough.

"You've got one-on-one in twenty minutes, my wild child. The first one-on-one is critical. I hacked your Intake. Your folks are insured to the gills. You could be in here past your child-bearing years. Hello!" Snap, snap. "You got to talk to Thurber. What have they got you on? Are you still peeing Thioridazine or what?" Snap, snap. "Wellburtin? Lithium? You got to pay attention to your meds."

Dani couldn't breathe. There *was* a blue room. And a bossy door. And this snapping, scratchy girl was the bossy door. The room started to sway.

"Look, nutbar, I'm trying to help." Snap, snap. "They're tying you to me, got it? Yolanda's convinced that I've got to get in touch with my inner girl scout before I can blow this place. Got it? Look, I know all your crap, and I still let them stick you with me. But there's a limit, ya know?" Snap, snap. "Hey, are you with me?" Snap. "I'm going to Spanish, and you're going to your gab-fest with Thurber, upstairs, Room 405." Snap, snap. "Hey! Daddy's girl!"

That was it.

In one perfect move, Dani got up and shoved Alison Hilary Mackenzie right into the dresser. Nail polish bottles clattered and tumbled every which way.

She had never touched anyone in anger in her life.

It was *so* not a nice thing to do, but . . . "Oh my God. . . . I'm so very . . ."

Scratch got up slowly and waved Dani off. "Okay," she said, stepping over the nail polish bottles. "Okay. So maybe I deserved that."

Dani combed through the alphabet, trying to form an apology by stringing the right combination of letters together. Except, the thing was, she didn't really feel sorry, really. What with all that bossing, teeth clenching, finger snapping—in fact, she felt pretty good and was still feeling pretty darned good when Scratch grabbed her by the shoulders. Picked her up. Threw her against the wall.

A picture frame fell. Glass shattered.

This Dani understood.

Scratch knelt down on one knee beside her. "Ground rules, princess. Even if I did deserve it, no one—and I mean absolutely no one—touches me. Ever. It's a thing, you know? You got a lot to learn. Are you going to be all—"

Just then there was a double knock on the door and a red-headed boy popped his head in. "Hey, Scratch. It's time for . . . uh-oh." He turned beet red. "Never mind. I can see you two are busy bonding." The door closed.

"Oh piss," groaned Scratch. "That was, uh, Kevin. I'll introduce you later." She disappeared into the bathroom.

Dani heard water running, followed by zealous splashing. She just sat on the floor replaying everything over and over again. What the heck happened here? Was it a good thing, a bad thing? What? She cradled the broken black and white woodcut of the Lady of the Lake grasping the sword Excalibur.

Scratch came out toweling her hands. "Uh . . . honors Spanish." She pointed toward the floor. "You're going up one floor to Room 405." She pointed toward the ceiling. "In twenty minutes. Got it?"

Dani hugged the frame tighter.

Scratch crouched down beside her again. "Look, you've got no reason to trust me. But," she shrugged, "what the hell. Trust me anyway. No one told me like I'm telling you. Talk to him. I'll hack into your meds chart and see what you're floating in, but in the meantime you got to talk to Thurber. Find a photo—even better, ask for the stupid photo album and make something up, or you'll be in here till you rot. I know. Just say words. Got it?"

Dani must have nodded or something because the next thing she knew she was alone. She crawled around gingerly picking up each glass shard and stacking them neatly in the garbage. Words. Okay. She looked up at the nail polish bottles. Did she like them largest to smallest or the other way around?

Words.

I can do words. I just about killed my roommate. Words'll be easy.

February 15, 9:35 A.M.

Dani was wobbly, but nothing hurt—much. She felt as if she was deep inside a cotton ball. Like the other times. Maybe it was an automatic type of thing. She smiled, pleased with herself. First day into the pen and already she was having major insights. At this rate she'd be out by the weekend.

When she was finally ready to leave the room, Dani noticed a folded piece of lined paper under the door. A big *"HI!"* was scrawled on the front. Her hands reached through the cotton-ball air to open the note.

> Okay, so her bite is even worse than her bark. Don't give up on Scratch just yet, she's actually a decent human person. Give her a chance. There, I said it. Destroy this note. Can't let it get out that I care. Catch ya later.
> Good Luck with Thurber!
> Kevin Faulkner (no, I'm not related to the writer)

Don't give up on Scratch? Shouldn't that be the other way

around? Kevin? The red-headed boy? What writer?

This place just couldn't get any weirder. She crumpled the note into a tight little ball and watched it swirl round and round the toilet bowl until it was finally sucked down.

The door to Room 405 was open. Dani clutched the yellow schedule sheet and knocked against the inside wall. "Uh . . ."

William Thurber pushed aside an unsteady chair and rose to greet her. "Come in, Danielle . . . sorry, Dani. Come in. Welcome."

This was her doctor? The Grand Pooh Bah? He looked like a king-size unmade bed.

"Make yourself comfortable—sit, sit, um, somewhere. . . ." He looked around his room accusingly.

Sit? Sit where? Dani followed his gaze. Impressive leather-bound books, files, magazines, brochures, and Taco Bell wrappers swallowed every available surface. Streaky mustard-colored walls fought against lumpy plaid furniture. She had to step over stuff. Dani had no idea that grown-ups actually lived this way.

You could perform open-heart surgery anywhere in Daddy's office.

"Oh . . ." Thurber shoved several color-coded file folders and magazines off a fraying wingback chair. "The place sometimes gets away from me. Sit down, relax. Please." He dug in behind the cushion and retrieved an October *Seventeen* magazine. He glanced at it before handing it to Dani. "I must have been keeping it for some profound reason, but," he shrugged, "here, I understand girls love to sneer at out-of-date fashion magazines."

Dani placed the magazine on her lap and tried to look

grateful, or at least not too alarmed.

"Well," he cleared his throat, "I'm your guy for the next little while."

He flashed her a smile. One of those whatchamacallit smiles where all the top teeth are showing like . . . Julia Roberts or . . . she couldn't think of anyone else, just Julia Roberts. He had nice teeth, too—straight, even, and a normal, healthy kind of white, not that blinding neon of her mother's lunch friends. Nice smile. You could never forget a smile like that.

"Of course, it's not like we haven't met already."

Oops.

He flipped through some papers. "Of course you can't be expected to remember my visits while you were nonresponsive in Isolation."

Nonresponsive. That didn't sound good. No siree. *Non*responsive.

"And your first day in the infirmary." He squinted at his notes. "I was just introducing . . ."

"I remember that!" Dani dove right in. "Sure, yeah. Well, some of it."

That smile again.

"That's great, Dani. We talked for a long time, or at least I did. I was one of the 'stethoscopes.'"

"Whoa, that came out loud?"

"Yes," he smiled again. "I thought it was pretty perfect. You're doing just fine." He started flipping through his files. "We—or I—reviewed your . . . uh . . . last visit to Westchester Emerg. The whole thing, the stomach pumping, alcohol poisoning, the prescription drugs . . . Should we go over that again, maybe?"

Why couldn't she remember anything? "Nope," she said. Why was she so retarded? This was nuts! "No, thanks. I got it nailed from the first time."

"Good." He stuffed an unlit cigarette into his mouth. "That's fine. I see that you've got Scrat . . . uh, Alison Mackenzie for a roommate. How is that going?"

"We're . . . uh . . ." Dani sank deeper into the chair. *Plays Well With Others* had to be real important in a place like this. "Good. We're . . . we're not giving up on each other."

"Excellent," he said. "She's an amazing kid." Thurber butted out the unlit cigarette and withdrew another one from the Marlborough pack on his window ledge. "Don't worry." He stuck another cigarette into his mouth and inhaled deeply. "I won't light up." He glanced at his watch. "I quit eleven days and three and a half hours ago."

Dani nodded. No question. She absolutely had to get out of here.

"Is there anything I can do to make you feel more comfortable?"

No, said Dani, but she forgot to say it out loud.

"You've had one heck of a journey these past few days. It has to have been terrifying. Do you have any questions about any aspect of being here? We're not taping today. We will in future though. I know it's old-fashioned, but I like to refer back to my tapes. Dani? It's a lot to take in. Do you have any concerns about being taped, any questions whatsoever?"

Questions? Yeah, of course. She must have a million questions. Lots of questions. About what though?

"It's probably still all too overwhelming right now."

One stinking question. Locked up in a nuthouse, and she didn't have any questions? Surely she could come up with one stupid . . . "Do you have any children?"

Thurber darkened and beamed at the same time. "Two boys, my miracles. I . . . um . . . share custody."

Stupid, stupid, stupid.

"Thanks for asking." Thurber fixed on her. "That was nice. Is there anything about your treatment, Dani, or that yellow sheet, your schedule? The staff maybe?"

Dani felt the panic rise up and clutch her throat so tight that none of the intelligent I'm-not-nuts questions could get through.

"Okay, then. Maybe later."

She was blowing it, not talking, not venting. He'd think . . . what? . . . something bad. Then she saw it. Beside the carton of Marlboroughs on the windowsill. Scratch was right. "Is that our photo album?"

Thurber crooked his eyebrow and swung his chair around. "Yes, Dani, it is. I asked your mother for it. You see, I believe that in certain circumstances, photographs can, well, help us see things that we didn't even know we were looking for."

"Mind if I look at it?"

He looked at her, then the album, then back at her. "Well, certainly. It's your photograph album." He placed it on top of the *Seventeen* magazine.

It felt like a fridge, that cold and that heavy. Thurber kept looking at her while he flicked invisible ashes into the ashtray.

Obligingly, she started flipping through the pages.

"In a few weeks, when you're ready, we'll start family therapy sessions, which will include your mother. Both Dr. Richardson and I have had a few conversations with her already. She's been right on top of all of this, Dani."

Good for her. Dani stopped at a page.

"It's very important that you understand that your father cannot come here. Ever. We kept trying to reassure you of that, but we weren't entirely sure about what you were taking in."

"I got that part," said Dani, stunned that the words came out and in the right order. Can't come here, no siree.

Thurber butted out another cigarette. Dani fixed on his hands. Big pawlike things. On his left ring finger was a thick white line where the ring used to live. It looked abandoned. She blushed and turned back to the photos.

"Most psychiatrists love this sort of thing," he smiled at her. "Is there anything you want to tell me about the photographs you're looking at?"

Dani shrugged. She hadn't really been looking at them.

"Any detail or feeling whatsoever that comes to mind?"

She frowned trying to concentrate. Fake pictures of fake people. The Ghost and her girls posing prettily at the base of the Statue of Liberty. Dani and Kelly slurping at their snocones.

"Dani, I can't help but notice that you keep returning to the picture of . . . uhmm," he got up and walked over to her, "of your family in front of that boat."

"Ferry."

"I stand corrected. Do you remember that day?"

It was a photograph of the four of them in front of the *Statue of Liberty Ferry.* Who took the photograph? Who were those people?

"Dani? You haven't left that picture. Do you remember that particular photo? I think your mother said that you were about five in all of these."

"We went to see the Statue of Liberty. To . . . uh . . . climb up, you know?"

"Uh-hmm. Dani, we'll have lots of time to wander around these pictures. Your body language altered at that page. Perhaps . . ."

Altered? She was sitting there gratefully holding a fridge in her lap. What the heck did this guy want?

"If you're not quite ready . . ."

"I'm ready already." She stared down at the page. Look at them. Her mother, so pale and perfect, fading already. Dani lingered over the suede hair band, navy blue twin set and crisp khakis. Kelly at two, almost the size of Dani, a rat's nest of bronze curls and a ripped DKNY sweatshirt. Daddy, blue jeans faded just so, blue jean shirt and a leather jacket carefully slung over his shoulder. God, was he really that beautiful? Daddy. And her . . . gripping Kelly. All of them smiling.

"Does anything come to mind when you look at that picture, Dani?"

Talk, speak, say anything. . . .

"They're a beautiful-looking family."

"They?"

"I mean, we. We're all so, uh . . . lovely. 'Course Kelly's kind of a mess, but we're pretty beautiful when you come right down to it."

"Anything else?"

Talk. Speak. Say something, you idiot cow.

That day, that day, that day. Dani remembered that day better than she remembered this morning.

Hot shame.

Oh God.

She had wet her pants on the ferry.

"Are you all right, Dani?"

Daddy was so wonderful about it on the ferry. Really, was there anyone more handsome? They all chuckled around him. Daddy wrapped his precious jacket around her waist. The jacket arms hugged her stomach, as warm and soft as butter. She was his princess. They all said so: "Beautiful child . . . what coloring . . . oh-h-h, she's too precious." They always said stuff like that wherever they went.

Thurber leaned over the photograph. "Are you troubled by the picture of the boat—I mean ferry—or something later at home?"

Home? Did she say that out loud? Later at home?

Thurber shredded a cigarette between his thumb and forefinger. "It's okay, Dani. Don't strain for the memory. We actually don't have to solve everything in the first session, no matter what you've heard."

She had ruined his jacket. She knew it. He didn't have to say. At five she knew about clothes, their clothes, the difference between Gucci and Prada. Mommy went to put Kelly down. And, unbelievably, Dani had to go again.

Thurber sat back on the window ledge, crossing his arms.

"It's early days yet. We may not even want to go exploring with photos. We may choose something else. Any number of alternative routes are open to us. We'll find the one that's most comfortable for you. Okay?"

Daddy marches her to the toilet. She pees again. Too many cherry snocones. Daddy stands there—right there—exactly there, watching. She sees that little muscle in Daddy's jaw go wild as he clenches and unclenches his teeth.

"Dani?"

She turns to flush, not breathing at all. Waiting. She reaches, but before she touches the handle, Daddy grabs the back of her head. Yanks her hair hard. "Ow! Daddy, ow!" Shoves her head into the toilet bowl. "Ow, Daddy!" She swallows. Her mouth is open. Drowning. Daddy, *no!* Da— Her mouth is open! Coughing, choking. Her mouth . . .

Then he flushes.

Dani clutched the photo album as if it were a life preserver.

"I had an accident."

Thurber glanced back at the photograph, puzzled. "That day?"

"No." She shook her head. "I broke a picture in our room. By accident. The Excalibur."

"I know the one." He said, tracking her. "It happens. Accidents happen all the time, Dani. They happen to everyone."

"Well, the glass, it went everywhere, but I think I got it all and put it into the garbage, you know. . . ."

"Good thinking." Thurber considered his lighter. "Hang on a minute." He picked up the phone and pressed two buttons. "Harold, Room 311, uh, a picture frame fell. There's glass shards in the . . ."

"Bathroom garbage," Dani mouthed.

"In the bathroom wastepaper basket. No. An accident, but do a sweep of the room. Sure." He nodded at the receiver and hung up. He glanced at the photos again, at the *Statue of Liberty Ferry* photo again. "Dani, we're still adjusting your meds. The exact dosage, the combinations, take quite some time to fine tune. Of course, they keep telling me not to tell you guys that." He grinned from ear to ear. "I just don't want you to feel bad. The medication levels could have a lot to do with memory function, with your ability to remember stuff, like that day."

That day. Dani gulped down the smell. Swallowed it. God, she had swallowed. It was in her, still to this day. Swallowed her own filth. What did he expect? Daddy's jaw muscle clenching and unclenching. That smell, she could smell it right then, weakness and urine. That's what shame smells like. She was full of it. The reek started to ooze out of her pores. Soon the office filled with it, pushing everything else out. And then it stopped, turned on a dime, and changed.

"Dani?"

Not that smell, but the other one, the old and powerful one pulsed through the shame. She waited, and it came. Sweet, pure cinnamon filled the room, caressed the air and devoured her.

William Thurber dropped his Marlborough. "Danielle? Is it the photo?" He began to scribble notes on a series of orange Post-It notes. "Dani?" He flicked the cigarette against the window and walked over to her. He checked her eyes and breathing. Then, ever so gently, he pried open her grip on the photo album to take her pulse. "Normal," he sighed. He crouched down and placed his hands on top of hers. "Where on earth did you go to?"

Twenty-One Months Ago

"Hey, Dani! Ready, all ready. Dani-i-i-i . . . any day now. . . . I said, ready, all ready. Did you get a concussion on the way down?"

The girls were at the bottom pitch of the ravine slope. Kelly was swiping twigs off her butt while Dani soaked in the smell of clean, black earth.

"Quit breathing like that. You're scaring me."

"Oh yeah?" Dani threw her arm around her sister's neck. "This better?" Kelly wriggled and struggled to get out of the headlock. "You see, Kelly, I can breathe weird and have a vision. And . . . I've got a beaut. Yuras has given Saraya some evil potion, so she's, like, awful confused and can't reach us like she used to. Genius?" She let Kelly go.

"Yeah, genius," Kelly groaned. "Excellent vision. You should hit your head on the way down more often. Still, vision or no vision, I'm captain. I called it first."

Dani started for a small clearing ringed by a circle of rocks. "You were captain last time."

Kelly loped after her. "Puhleeze! I feel awesome clues coming on. I can almost feel where Yuras has the Goddess stashed. Please, ple-e-e-ze. . . ."

Kelly always got to be captain.

"Pretty puh-le-e-e-ze."

Dani didn't mind, just pretended to. What she hated was the pleading. The incessant buzzing, like a fly trapped in a pot. If she ever whined like that, Daddy would've . . . "Okay, Kelly, but just this once."

"Yes!" burst Kelly as she tripped over one of the circle rocks.

"For Godsake, Kelly! A little decorum please. We are at the Sacred Portal."

"Sorry, sorry. Got it?"

Dani nodded and they moved to face each other. They were almost at eye level now. Toes to toes, freckles to freckles. Dani reached into the side leg pocket of her cargo pants and pulled out a perfect double scrolled cinnamon stick. Kelly clasped the other end, and they bowed their heads and prayed.

We call on Saraya.
Goddess hear our prayer.
Hold back the darkness.
Grant us strength to bear.
Grant us your light through fog and shame.
Grant us forgiveness, when we waiver and wane.
Stay with us, Saraya.
Unlock the key.
Stand by us, Saraya.
We will set you free.

Breathing in perfect time, they snapped the cinnamon scroll in two and crushed it. Pieces of broken cinnamon bark chewed their fingertips until they were smothered in the scent.

"Are we in?" Kelly asked, eyes shut tight. "Did it work? Tell me the colors. Are they Game colors?"

Dani looked up and around, grabbing pieces of sky. She was hypnotized by the sunlight. Game sunlight, the kind that eats through the air and fires up all the new grass. She was stunned all over again. It had worked. She could still bring it off. She could almost convince herself that it was real.

"Behold, Captain!" Dani waved dramatically at a tree. "The maple shoots are glistening emeralds, and a million bluebells blaze in sapphire glory on the northern edge. Every single shade and tone is so clear and sharp, you could cut yourself on the color. We made it through the portal of our mind's eye. We have entered the Game."

Kelly's eyes brightened. "Ooooo, that's good." She nodded feverishly. "I see all that. Great entry. Yup."

"I aim to please." Dani bowed. "Today I feel we must search for clues and portents of where the evil one has stashed . . . uh . . . imprisoned the Goddess. The signs are everywhere, but we've been blind or something, okay? Got it? How's that?"

"Excellent, perfect . . . got anything else?" asked Kelly.

"Maybe later," Dani shrugged. "I'm kind of tired. Don't take this captain stuff so seriously, for Godsake." She started for the field at the opposite slope with Kelly bounding up behind her. This part of the ravine floor was smothered in tall blue grasses. It was like walking through the ocean. Dani began pulling up shoots and braiding them into a headband.

"That is so cool. Do me one? Hey, it could be part of our armor! What do you think?"

"Not bad," nodded Dani. "The headbands could make us invincible. Yeah. Invincible is a very good thing to be."

"Exactly!" Kelly sprang at her sister. "It's too perfect. No one will see us. Sometimes those stupid joggers . . ."

"Not invisible, dufus, invincible—untouchable, unhurtable."

"Even better! It'll make us brave and brilliant so we can find the Goddess no matter where he's stuck her. And when we set her free, we'll hunt him down like a dog and then we'll . . . uh . . . what's that word for kill off?"

"Vanquish," said Dani. "Same thing, but it means we'll kill him in a really elegant and glorious sort of way."

"Yeah. I knew that. We'll vanquish him to a pulp."

"Come here." Dani wrapped the grass headband around her sister's forehead. "That's what he needs all right, a good vanquishing." She cast about and headed toward the bluebells, pulling Kelly along with her. "This'll be perfect!" She threaded the tiny little blossoms into Kelly's headband.

"And then when we're done vanquishing Yuras, we can go after Daddy, right?" Whenever Kelly got a little nervous, her voice raised in pitch.

"Stop it, Kelly."

"Only after we're done with Yuras. I mean, there's got to be something—"

"Stop it. I'm tired. I said I was tired before. So don't keep pushing!"

"Why are you so tired all the time?"

Kelly's voice pierced in and behind Dani's eye where the headaches lived. The flies were buzzing again.

"You're always so tired. It's not fair. Tired, tired, tired. If you weren't so tired, I bet you'd figure something out about Da—"

"Shut up!" Dani grabbed her sister's shoulders. "If you'd quit pissing up your bed at night maybe I wouldn't be so tired. Who the heck cleans up, huh? Who's the one who gets nailed for *your* little problem?"

Kelly's eyes welled up. She was afraid. Afraid of Dani?

Dani's shame blanketed every sound in the ravine. It muffled the breeze, the bluejays, her sister crying.

"Dani." Tears raced out of Kelly. "Oh, Dani, I'd do anything. I'm such a . . . sorry, sorry. I don't do it on purpose. I can't help . . . I know you . . ."

Before her head could explode, Dani grabbed her sister, clutching her tight against her. "Sh-h-h-h-h, I know, I know. I didn't mean it. That was bad. I'm the one that's bad. Sh-h-h-h, Kelly, sh-h-h-h." She wiped her sister's face with her sleeve. "Sh-h-h-h."

"Don't say that!" Kelly snuffled. "You're not bad. It was Yuras. He's, like, seeping through or something. You're brilliant and awesome and good."

Kelly's poor headband was coming apart and tilting at a rakish angle; bluebells were everywhere. Dani tried not to laugh. "You're right, Kelly. It was the evil one speaking. We vanquish Yuras, we vanquish the evil, right?"

Kelly snuffled and nodded.

"I'll always take care of you. You know that, don't you?"

"I know, Dani." Kelly vacuumed back her runny nose and

got a bluebell stuck up her nostril.

Dani pretended not to see it. "So, Captain, I await your battle plan."

Kelly tried to snort out the bluebell but started laughing, which just sucked the flower up more. That was it. Kelly passed into that twilight zone of laughter. Nobody laughed like Kelly. It came from deep down in her toenails. You couldn't be within earshot of her and not laugh, too. So they both lost it, giggling and snorting, which led to Kelly farting. "For Godsake, can't you figure out how to laugh and not fart at the same time?" Eventually, Kelly seemed to remember the dignity of her office, and after extended throat clearing, she announced her plan.

"Well, I bid us to go forth to the . . . uh, the Elfin stream. That's it! I can feel it."

The girls swam out of the long grasses and tried to pick out an overgrown footpath.

"Dani, tell me about before . . . you know, when Mom was . . . before . . ."

"Kelly." They were marching in single file.

"Before she became the Ghost. You know, in the old backyard, like when we were really little."

Dani pretended not to hear.

"And we'd play in the piles of leaves, you said, and dance around with Mom. She'd sing, you said. You said she always sang this song all the time. How come she loved that song so much?"

Dani marched faster.

"It's not fair, Dani." Now she was yelling. "You know I can't hardly remember." The ravine reverberated with her shouting.

"It's just not fair! All I've got is your remembering to remember."

"Ae-a-r-r-g-h-h! Okay, okay." Dani turned around. "Mom used to say that when she was a little kid, she watched this old TV show with Gran." Kelly nodded like it was the first time she had ever heard any of this. "And so, anyway, this guy, the host, would sing 'Lavender's Blue.' I forget what it's really called, and Mom and Gran would sit there on Granny's green plaid couch singing along."

"And . . ."

"And she'd say that nothing but nothing ever made her feel so safe as sitting on the couch with Gran and listening to that stupid song except—"

"Except when she sang it to us," Kelly finished. "And then?"

"And then she just didn't sing it anymore, period. Okay? Quit asking about that part like the ending is going to change."

"Sing it, Dani."

"Oh, man."

"Puh-le-e-e-ze, Dani."

"Okay, okay. Don't whine, for Godsakes."

Kelly walked backward, waiting for Dani to start. Dani rolled her eyes and obliged. Kelly knew the words even better than she did, but it didn't seem to count unless someone sang it to her.

Lavender's blue, dilly dilly
lavender's green.
When I am king, dilly dilly . . .

Once adequately jump-started, Kelly was happy to belt out the rest on her own. When she had wrestled the song to its conclusion, Kelly jumped onto the nearest boulder. "You were right, Dani. I do feel it."

"What?" Her sister looked demented bopping around on the boulder, trying to enlist all the birds and squirrels in her quest. "What do you feel?"

"Our magic will indeed run high today."

"Good," Dani bowed deeply. "Then by all means lead on, dear Captain."

February 22

Dear Kelly,

Hi Kiddo. Sorry I didn't write earlier, I didn't know if I could. I mean, I knew they'd let me, but I didn't know if I could, you know? Anyway, okay, so I really blew it. I don't know what they told you but you know not to believe them just on principle, right???

The thing is, or was, I had another boo-boo so, apparently, I had the old stomach pumped again. The other thing is that instead of bringing me home and taking care of me, Mommy dearest locks me up! Perfect, huh, just like in the movies. But the weirdest thing is that I just don't know, you know? Like, there are times when I honestly don't know if I'm really nuts and should be grateful to be in here or if I'm mainly okay and they're just making me nuts with all their drugs and stuff. It sort of depends on which five-minute cycle you catch me in. One thing for sure is that absolutely everyone else in this place is rowing with one oar out of the water.

I've met a bazillion people but I keep getting them mixed up. Or maybe it's just one person with a lot of different personalities. I think that there really is someone running around here like that. See what I mean? When I get it straight I'll fill you in. You'd love it. Well, not love it, but you'd love meeting them. Okay, maybe you wouldn't love meeting them so much as . . . earghh! It's got some interesting bits, you know. I keep thinking how you'd turn this all into a great story. I would too if only it weren't my story. Anyway, the first person I remember clearly is Yolanda L. Briggs (none of us know what the L. stands for), the head nurse who is the size of a small country. So's this guy Harold, who's like the supervising orderly/Master of the Universe. Harold eats Hell's Angels for breakfast and . . . then there's my shrink, Dr. William Thurber. He too is bigger than a building. Do you sense a pattern here or is it just me???? I'd tell you more, except my opinions seem to be on the same five-minute cycle my memory's on.

I have a couple of friends. Well, not friends so much maybe, but they let me hang with them, you know? What I mean is, I don't think they hate me, not even Scratch. She's my roommate, Alison Hilary Mackenzie. Scratch insists that everybody call her "Scratch" and for good reason, let me tell you. She's one of those self-mutilator types. What did I tell you? Like, how weird is that? Even weirder is that she's like the cool kid of the nuthouse. Pretty well everyone's afraid of her except for Kevin who's a real sweetie.

They both think I should yak it up more. See, my brilliant strategy, and you'll recognize this one, is not to talk about anything just in case it's not the drugs, you know? I figure if I keep my mouth shut maybe it won't be so noticeable that I really do belong in a place like this. It works fine except for Scratch who thinks it sucks as a plan and I'll never see the light of day if I keep up. Like she's an authority on "normal." This from a chick who slices and dices!

The main thing is I *have not* abandoned you! You've got to know that. I'll do whatever they want me to and I'll come back as soon as I can figure out how. Got it? But in the meantime you have got to remember not to . . . you know, have an accident while I'm in here. I can't fix it from here. Do the alarm thing like I showed you when my class went to Washington. That worked, right? You set it every hour . . . maybe even every forty-five minutes . . . heck, stay up all night if you have to. If an accident happens, don't let yourself fall back asleep!!! I've been giving this a lot of thought. You strip the bed and quietly take it all to the dryer. Don't bother with the washing machine—too loud. Twenty minutes and, poof, put it back. Deal with the mattress when he's gone in the morning. Do whatever you have to. I get nuts thinking about him finding out. Actually that's not true, mostly I'm so scared for me that there's not a whole lot of room to be scared for you too. I work you in when I can. Ha!!

Write right away, tell me not to worry, and blah blah blah, okay? Don't bother worrying about me. I've been through worse. I'll be okay. Okay? Just write, like RIGHT NOW PICK UP A PEN. Hey, I just read this letter over and if

I didn't know any better I'd swear this was a decent sort of normal letter-writer person. See, I'll be out in a minute. Hang tough kid. We'll vanquish Yuras yet.

Love (and I mean it)

Dani

P.S. Burn this. Like right now!

February 22, 1:50 p.m.

"Whatchya doing, writing a journal?" asked Scratch. She'd torn herself away from her meticulous toenail polishing to squint suspiciously at Dani, who was hunched over the desk at the far side of their room. Scratch's toes were an intensive production. Not content with any of the shades in her nail polish collection, Scratch painstakingly created her own by mixing, matching, blending, and cursing. She never embarked on this journey without first sticking monster pink foamy things between her toes, which splayed them so far apart she looked like a demented frog. "They love you to write journals. You get major points for it. I'd mention it to Thurber or at least Yolanda." She sighed deeply. "It could help counteract your whole too-stupid-for-words routine of not talking."

Dani stared at the paper. "No, it's a letter." She glanced at Scratch's spectacular toes. "To Kelly." She waited for some kind of response from her roommate. None came. She could hear Scratch breathing, or was that her? "She's my sister."

"I know that. . . . Damn it."

"What?" Dani licked her lips and tasted fear. "What?"

"Nothing . . . uh . . . the shade." Scratch got up and duck-walked over to the dresser. "I don't think this creation says *me* enough." She examined her bottles. "Ah-h! All it needs is an overlay of Garbage Gold. What do you think?"

Dani had never been allowed to wear anything but clear nail polish. "Sure, well, yeah." She glanced back at their alarm clock. "Don't we have to go now?" It was going to be Dani's first Little Group session.

"Relax, Sherlock." Scratch hobbled back to her bed with the polish. "We've got loads of time. Are you still freaked about Little Group?"

Dani turned her chair around to face Scratch. "No." She hugged herself. "Hey, I've had my stomach pumped. Twice. I figure group therapy will feel like the third time. Everybody in that room will be crawling around my insides and making judgment calls on the contents. What's to freak out about?"

"They're not all like me, Cinderella." Scratch unplugged her toes and tossed the foamies at Dani. "I keep telling you it's not like that. You have to manage the whole thing. Manage, manage, and then manage some more." Scratch used new foamy things for every single pedicure, which was almost every single day.

Dani was in awe of someone who would even know where to buy stuff like that, let alone what to do with it once it was home.

"Okay, listen to Mama. First of all, it's easier to score points if you say something. . . ."

Dani shook her head.

"But . . . it's not as critical in Little Group as it is in one-on-one or in parent meetings, at least in the beginning. Thing is . . ."

Dani nodded, waiting.

"Thing is, you got to look like you're paying attention. Empathize. Don't look at someone blankly like you're doing now."

"I've been practicing sincere empathy."

Scratch looked alarmed. "That's empathy? Hmmm, try nodding slowly like you can't get over what was just said, but you know it's true."

Dani nodded and tried to look pained at the same time.

"Better," said Scratch. "And every so often, look shocked or indignant. Doesn't really matter when. And then finally . . . when all else fails, blank nod."

"Blank nod?" Dani nodded.

"Blank nodding is like you're barely there. Whatever was said has just thrown you deep into a personal memory. Good nodding is everything."

Dani nodded, stunned.

"Just pay close attention to Kevin and me."

As if on cue, there was a double knock on the door. "Are you two ripping each other's entrails out, or can I come in?"

"Piss off, Kevin," yelled Scratch.

He took that as sign of welcome, waltzed in, and winked at Dani before sitting beside Scratch. He whistled at her feet. "Too gross for words, dear."

"You are absolutely the only queer in the entire country without any sense of style." Scratch stuck her tongue out at him.

"That, dear heart, is racist," he frowned. "Or sexist. Or at the very least, it's a cliché. As if you could even spell the word *style.* I mean, my God, two-year-old GAP sweats!" He made a face as he fingered Scratch's outfit *du jour.*

Dani marveled at the two of them all over again. Sometimes she was intimidated by them, and sometimes she just didn't get them at all, but she loved floating in their orbit.

Kevin waved at Scratch's feet. "Are those things dry? We got to go, pumpkin."

Scratch popped off the bed. "I'm going barefoot."

"Uh . . ." offered Dani.

"Take a Valium, will you." She headed for the bathroom. "Yolanda's off, Harold's at Isolation all day, and everyone else worships me. I'll just wash up."

Kevin took a step over to her. "Scratch . . ."

"What? I'm dirty." She slid into the bathroom.

"Well, aren't your feet going to get all dirty?"

By the stunned way Kevin looked at her, Dani assumed that those words must have come out of her.

"See, Kevin, my boy," Scratch called out over the rushing water, "I told you it talks."

Kevin made a face, making sure he caught Dani's eye. "I suppose when you're as deranged as she is, dirty feet are a major milestone." He blushed.

Dani had never seen a guy blush before.

Scratch swooped them both up on her way out of the bathroom. "Let's go, children. My audience awaits."

Dani hovered just inside the doorway to the small boardroom. The room was so . . . white. The walls were white, the floor was white, the ceiling . . . too bright. Somebody, a girl, was pulling down old-fashioned roller blinds on the windows. The sun filtered through, softening everything, making the room bearable. A dozen or so molded metallic chairs were placed in a sloppy circle. Vaguely familiar-looking kids were strewn around the circle. She watched as Scratch sidled up to a nervous-looking boy whose name, Dani thought, was Bobby something.

"Hey, Bobo. How's it hanging?"

The poor guy looked stricken, but then he brightened. "Hey, Scratch. They're hanging low today."

Scratch rewarded him with a smile. "Atta go, Bobo. Consider yourself hugged."

It was like someone had just handed him a puppy.

A few more kids streamed in. Dani listened greedily as they called out to one another. William shuffled in, his hands bandaged with gauze. He was followed by Agnes, whom you could see through. Both of them sat across from Kevin. A boy named Sam stomped in manically playing an invisible guitar. Nobody greeted him.

She didn't belong here.

She couldn't belong here.

Dani was still considering where to sit when she heard a girl screeching outside the room. "Please, baby. It won't happen again." Someone swathed in black spandex from head to toe was mincing and whimpering all the way up the hall toward the boardroom. "Jared, baby . . . wait up. Ba-a-a-a-by."

She didn't notice him until he was almost on top of her, against her, breathing on her.

"O-o-o-o-o, fresh meat."

Dani willed herself to look at him, into deep blue, bruised eyes. His breath came at her in waves of spearmint. Everything else disappeared. His expression didn't change as he reached for her. He squeezed her breast so hard that Dani thought she was going to pass out—faint in the middle of all that spearmint. Did anyone see? Was anyone . . . ? His hand was a vise. Dani gasped and inhaled at the same time. Finally, she fell against the wall. The room swam in front of her.

"Don't be ashamed, honey," he flicked his tongue. "I like 'em little."

Was he was going to lick her face?

Suddenly, chairs crashed, and Kevin and Scratch were by her side. Everyone was standing.

"Hey, puke face!"

Jared turned to Scratch, who took the opportunity to nail his left eye with a big wad of spit. "Get your diseased paws off her."

Scratch looked quizzically at Dani, searching. Dani searched back.

Jared didn't blink as he reached for Kevin's arm and wiped his face with Kevin's sleeve. "Whatsa matter, razor girl? She yours?"

"That's right, armpit."

By now the spandex girl, Janice, was pleading and tugging at Jared's arm. Scratch's face had turned into concrete. She leaned into Jared and whispered, "Keep at it and I'll get you back into F Ward before you take your next crap. *Sit down, Jared."*

Pow, it was all over.

The boy allowed himself to be coaxed to a seat by Janice. He was as gentle as a lamb.

Dani sat between Kevin and Scratch. Chairs were put back and Thurber turned up dragging his wonky office chair and apologizing for his tardiness. Greetings all around. Introductions, stories, arguments. They smiled. She smiled.

Every so often, Scratch nudged her and Dani nodded, a nice, empathetic nod.

Or so they told her afterward.

She remembers at some point sitting there, warm and safe, bookended by Kevin and Scratch. She did not look at Jared. She also remembers not being able to take her eyes off the bank of windows just behind Thurber and the bandaged-up William. All the blinds were shabby and worn. Like her, they didn't belong in that pristine, surgical room. But then again, they did. She did. Near the top of the middle bank of windows, way up, someone had scratched through one of the blinds.

How?

At first, it looked like crazy little random rips. Then the sun moved, and soft marmalade rays shone through the etchings. She remembers that she turned her head, squinting just so, and, finally, unbelievably, was able to decipher the secret, illuminated words. Someone had somehow managed to scratch into the fabric, "Please Help the Blind."

She remembers laughing out loud.

Dr. William Thurber March 3
Clinical Director
Riverwood Youth Clinic
Riverwood, New York
10621

Dear Dr. Thurber,

I feel I have to thank you again for being so patient with me last week. As you know, I've been seeing Dr. Richardson regularly, and I'm more at peace with my decision to hospitalize Dani. However, coming to terms with what necessitated that decision, well, "one step at a time," as they say.

I must reiterate that you needn't concern yourself over Mark's latest legal threats or our financial obligations to the clinic. I also know that, court order or not, Mark will make every effort to see her. On top of everything else his reputation is at stake and, well, I am fully confident in your ability to keep him at bay. On a more positive note, I flew home over the weekend and explained the whole sorry mess to my father. Anyway, my father has undertaken to set up a living trust which should see us through all of Dani's immediate and post-clinic care, as well as our upcoming custody issues. I'm no longer above accepting a little guilt money. Another miracle is that I've found part-time employment as an interior decorator at a firm we've used for years. When Dani comes out of this, she won't be able to stop laughing.

I realize that I've made quite a nuisance of myself. At this point, I'm grateful that you even return my calls. I do completely, totally understand about the visitations, and I agree that the issue should not in any way be forced. Dani will see me when she is able to, period. That's fine, but I have to keep coming. I don't mind waiting in the commons, just in case. You never know.

Sincerely,
Sandra Webster

MARCH 21

Dani slammed the door so hard, all of her key chains popped off their perch on the dresser mirror. She stomped over and glared at the mirror. Scratch, who was sprawled on her bed, loomed large in the reflection. She continued gleefully blacking out teeth on the models in her *Vogue* magazine.

"Rough day at the office, Dani boy?"

Dani piled up errant key chains and tossed them onto her half of the dresser. Scratch's half was crowded, too, but meticulously crowded. Crammed against all the nail polishes were perfect little stacking bins lined with nail accessories, makeup brushes and sponges of every size and description. Who knew that Q-tips came in more than one size? Dani's half had two pens and all the key chains that her mother had sent over. As a presence, she was invisible in the rest of the room. Scratch's cleansing and soothing products dominated every available surface, including the window wells and radiator covers, while fashion magazines grew in tidy, square piles on the floor.

Dani growled at her own reflection. "Richardson was there."

"O-o-o-o." This caught Scratch's attention. She sat up. "Number Two Pooh Bah was there with Number One Pooh Bah? Hmmn. Full court press. What do they want you to do?"

Dani continued to peer at her roommate through the mirror. "They're . . . he's turning on the screws for me to see my mother, who apparently haunts the commons room." It was bizarre watching herself talk while she checked Scratch for reactions. Her roommate looked bored again. "And Richardson kept pressing his point that I'm way past due for a couple of sessions with dear old Mom, let alone a visit."

Scratch went back to her magazine. "And did you say anything about any of this? Out loud, I mean, so that regular human-type people could hear?"

"Yeah." Dani continued to gaze at herself. When was the last time she looked in a mirror? Her hair was growing out. Good. Definitely no bare bits left. Now, if she could just remember chopping it off.

"Yeah what?"

"Well," Dani turned around and crossed her arms, "maybe I said something like I wouldn't be in here in the first place if it wasn't for the queen of the Stepford Wives."

"Atta pick your moment to emote." Scratch rolled her eyes. "I'm sure they've both seen the movie. It's such a classic."

Dani shrugged.

"I don't know why you're standing around. Get your gear together. They must be signing your exit papers as we speak."

"Don't!" Dani fell onto her bed. "Don't. I know I blew it. So now what?"

"Well, that's something at least. Look, you can't keep being such a jerk about this. Do you think they're ever going to let you out of here while you're still refusing to see your old lady? Like, how bright is that, Sherlock?"

"Like you give a . . . couldn't you shut up with your expert opinion for once!"

Scratch snapped the magazine shut. "Did-you-or-did-you-not-ask?" She said this very slowly.

The words hung in the air with nowhere to go. Dani picked at her T-shirt. "I . . . sorry. I was always the one with the answers, the one who does the taking care of." She shuddered. "I'm as much a pain to you as Kelly is to . . ."

"Oh, man." Scratch began fingering her assortment of body lotions. "You're not that much of a pain. I mean, not that you're not a pain, but a bearable pain, okay? Low-grade headache tops. Besides, I don't have a little sister." Scratch squeezed on some Roses and Rosemary. "I've been in here since God was a boy, and before here, other places." She massaged the lotion into her hands like it was the most important thing in the world. "Lots of other places. Don't do as I did, Dani. Do as I say. You've got to start talking out there, and you've got to see your old lady. Do you want to get out of here and take care of . . . of stuff, or not?"

"Why didn't you warn me about Jared?"

"Whoa, is that still eating your ass?" Scratch threw the hand lotion at Dani. "I told you a million times. We thought he was in F Ward, permanent like. He deserves to be. He was caught using in here. Look, the rumor is that his old lady is screwing one of the clinic's board of directors. Maybe even the chairman."

She made a face. "Although I've actually seen that guy, and there's no way I think he could get it up, so . . ."

Dani didn't know where to look. She didn't want to deal with that picture in her head.

"Anyway, cool your jets. I'll figure out how to get him back in there. It just takes a little time. I told you all this, didn't I?"

"Yeah, you did," Dani nodded. "Just checking, I guess. I was kind of wobbly back then." She turned around. "Thanks, Alison."

Silence filled the space between them and pushed.

"That's Scratch to you."

Dani got up, opened her mouth, thought better of it, closed it, and sat down again. "Why?" She turned to her roommate. "Why is it Scratch to me? Why is it Scratch to anyone?"

"O-o-o-o-o, what to do, what to do? She scores with a direct question about a clearly loaded topic. Hmmm, I could either reward you or put you through the shredder. Let's see . . ."

"No, really. I mean it." Dani inhaled. "You've read all my charts and stuff. You probably know more about me than I do. I just want to know this one thing about you."

"You're lucky that I have this soft spot for kids with psychopathic daddies." Scratch stared at the wallpaper like she'd never seen it before. The silence pushed harder this time. "I had to be first in, you know?"

Dani shook her head.

"Breathe out, Dani. You got to get that breathing thing together. They notice little details like that." She went back to the wall. "Anyway, that was the last time I looked. Understand? I mean, really, really looked. I guess, I still look but I don't see anymore? Do you get that at all?"

Dani shrugged. "I don't think I saw myself too clearly the night I chopped off my hair." She smiled at Scratch. "You have beautiful hair. Almost bronzy, right? Like Kelly's, except hers is a mess. Yours is nice and shiny."

"Yeah. Uh . . . thanks. Stay with me now, okay? We're not doing a Clairol commercial. Anyway, so . . . so . . . I looked, and I saw that one time and well. See, it's all over my arms, my shoulders, quite a bit on my stomach. . . ." Scratch shut her eyes. "I looked like a crumpled paper bag full of broken glass. Scratch. Scratch. So . . ."

Dani didn't blink.

"Like I said, I don't see anymore. Once was enough. Anyway, I knew I had to get it in there before anyone else did, and *voilà*, Scratch was born." She glanced at Dani for a reaction.

Dani folded and refolded her sweating hands.

"Thurber says a lot will fade. Then there's lasers and stuff when I'm ready. *Ready,* Dani. Big little word *ready* is." She took her eyes off the wallpaper and turned back to Dani. "At least she comes, kiddo. Your old lady is out there every single sunny day. She's going to redecorate the frigging lounge if you don't go see her."

Dani nodded at her hands.

"I swear you want to get slugged!" Scratch heaved a pillow at her. Without missing a beat, Dani heaved it back, plus thwacked her with her own.

Within seconds they were screaming and beating each other senseless with pillows and assorted bedding. Dani was gasping, "Uncle, uncle!" when they both fell into the dresser. The key chains went flying all over the place.

"What the hell is it with you and these things?" Scratch pulled out a miniature soccer ball from under her butt.

Dani retrieved roving little Minnie Mouse, Daffy Duck, the mini etch-a-sketch, and a rabbit's foot. "I . . . uh . . . collect key chains."

"Ah-h-h-h . . . well, that explains it then, doesn't it?" She crossed her eyes at a miniature Cruella De Vil. "We really got to work harder on the talking thing. See, I say or ask something remarkable or revealing, and without pausing, you sally back with something equally remarkable or revealing."

"Okay, okay. I started years ago. Mother bought me a little Jack Frost in a teeny glass globe with the real fake snow that shakes and everything. I think it was from a movie promotion." She plucked another escaped figurine from under the bed. "Well, Kelly broke it. Probably by accident. I think."

"Yeah, kids," said Scratch.

"Anyway, by then I already had dozens and dozens and I love every single one and they all have their own personality so I always carry at least five on my back pack and interchange them weekly so they don't get jealous, I mean, so nobody feels left out is what I really mean." She was as red as a beet.

"Exhale, Dani. And when you're talking, I'd recommend thinking in terms of commas and periods, the whole grammatical menu."

"Right." She took a few deep breaths, counting out beats. "Anyway, the one I always keep with me no matter what, is him, see?" She held out the escaped key chain, an oblong bubble. Dani beamed at the little old sailor encased inside. "See? He's wearing a yellow anorak and doesn't his face look like a raisin? A happy raisin. And look, he's always rowing his beaten up old dinghy. He never stops no matter what. The Old Man and the Sea." She remembered to stop and breathe some more. "My, uh . . . daddy . . . would sometimes, when the mood hit him, try to do father-like stuff, which usually meant that he would read his favorite books to us." She took a gulp of air. "What a joy. You could pound the air with a meat cleaver. But sometimes . . . he could be so . . . well, anyway, I fell in love with The Old Man and the Sea."

"Which, your key chain or the Hemingway fisherman?"

"Both. Well, actually I loved the fish, too. Then out of the blue, Daddy came home from a conference with him. Saw him in a kiosk in San Francisco and brought him back. For me." She cradled the plastic bubble tenderly. "Go figure."

Scratch nodded. Dani had unleashed more words in this one afternoon than all the weeks that they had roomed together.

"I love him even more than Trusty Troll." She held up a filthy plastic troll with fried orange hair.

"What happened to him?"

"Oh, he was regular sacrifice material in the, this . . . game we used to play."

"Dani, breathe out. In, then out. You know the drill. Pay attention to your breathing. Not breathing is sort of a nuts thing to do. It's right up there with not talking."

"Right. I'm out of practice, I guess. On the talking part." She inhaled and then exhaled smartly. "The, uh, breathing thing is . . . so, thing is, I want you to have him, the Old Man and the Sea, I mean."

"Huh?"

Dani thrust the fisherman into Scratch's hands. "He holds the most magic of all of them, and he'll keep you company no matter what or where. You know, when I'm gone."

"Well, I wouldn't go packing any bags just yet."

"He's very gentle and he's a good listener. Please?"

Scratch cupped the torn-up bubble like it was an egg ready to hatch. She squinted at Dani, trying to decipher the indecipherable. "Thanks. But don't think that just because I take him I'm going to feel obligated to go all adorable or anything."

Dani hugged herself.

"Yeah, well." Scratch got up and pointed to the washroom. "Okay then, how's about we celebrate this emotional breakthrough by you having a shower and . . . what the heck, let's go for a change of clothes?"

"Okay, okay, okay," Dani groaned. "I give up." She went to the bathroom and shut the door.

"Feel free to dip into my White Ginger gels, foam, and shampoo." Scratch's muffled voice seeped through the door. "They're great after a workout."

Dani rolled her eyes.

"Or the Luscious Lemon stuff is equally soothing and refreshing."

Dani squirted a bit of both into the tub and immediately craved Chinese takeout. "Thanks. It's . . . uh . . . delicious." She heard a bonk against the bathroom door. "What?"

"Dani, you can do it. You're ready. She always waits for such a long time."

Dani roared the hair dryer into action and then turned it right off. What was the point? Her hair still wasn't more than an inch long even at its longest bits.

"Every single visitors' day for, like, the whole afternoon. She's creeping everybody out."

Dani stared at the bathroom door. She could almost feel Scratch lying against it, sort of like that first time.

"Dani!?"

"Yeah?"

"Well, it means dick all to me and all, but . . ."

"Yeah?"

". . . at least she comes."

March 21, 4:00 p.m.

Her mother strode toward her, bristling with efficiency. Dani held her ground, trying not to shake, or at least not to shake noticeably. Her mother looked as if she was going to march right up to a Junior League podium and thank everyone for coming.

Instead, she embraced Dani.

Almost.

They didn't hug like other people. Dani knew the difference. Images of people embracing in doorways, bus terminals, and even here in the commons, seared her. Bodies would careen, dissolving and melting into warm, outstretched arms. Other people would greet each other with loud, thumping bear hugs. Dani ached for one of those "other people's hugs."

She didn't ask.

It would be begging.

She knew not to beg.

So their arms circled, searched, but didn't quite touch. It was a germ-free hug. Out of sheer force of habit, she kissed her mother's cheek. As always it was like kissing Kleenex. Actually, not "always," but Dani couldn't really and truly remember the times before "always." They were just stories she trotted out to make Kelly happy.

"Well . . ." Her mother broke the circle, ironing out invisible creases in her luncheon suit. She examined Dani without making eye contact. "Well, darling! I'm just so very, very delighted that you're up to a visit. I can't possibly begin to express what this means to me."

Dani wondered if her mother had come so immaculately turned out every single time. What did she do while she waited? Did she hang with the guys in the TV lounge? Dani swallowed a giggle, imagining her mother pruning decaying rubber plants and plumping up vinyl pillows. What did she make of Jared, who liked to "rearrange" himself in front of an audience, preferably in front of someone else's parents?

"Truly, so terribly grateful, I can't begin to tell you. Is there anything you need? Anything I can get . . . ?"

Dani's laughter erupted so violently that she startled the ardent TV fans mesmerized by Vanna White blithely turning over letters on the lounge's giant screen. Kevin was among them. She knew that in a moment of weakness he had promised Scratch that he'd "spot" Dani's first visit. Her laugh was wrong, way off; even she could hear it. Kevin swiveled his chair around for a peek. He looked startled by them. Why?

"Hell, no!" Dani was flinging her arms around the corridor. "I'm in a nuthouse. What more could a kid ask for? I'm sure there's another award in this for you."

Her mother flinched, but you'd have to have been an expert to catch it.

"Darling. Dani please. I know. . . . Please, let's not make this more brutal than it already is. Perhaps we could sit?"

"I want to stand!" Dani was shouting. *"I like standing!"* Why was she shouting? *"Why can't I stand?!"* She never shouted at her mother, never shouted at anyone. She was a shouting, hitting fool. Stupid, stupid. They might as well throw away the key.

She felt Kevin's eyes on her, imploring her.

"Of course, darling. Anything . . ." Her mother reached over and touched her cheek. Dani felt the fingers burn and swatted them away. Her mother stepped back.

Mrs. Webster jerked awkwardly. It was as if she was trying to figure out what to do with her hands, her purse, her posture all at once. She returned to ironing her skirt. "On a brighter note, darling, I'm very happy to hear that whatever contretemps you had with your roommate seems to be resolved. Dr. Thurber and Dr. Richardson both tell me that you and—Alison is it?—have become fast friends. In fact . . ."

Dani strained to pay attention, but her head kept tabulating mistakes to date. Shouldn't have slapped her hand away. Why did her mother touch her? Okay. Okay. Get a grip. No shouting, no laughing. Must stop acting like I belong here, for Godsake.

"Now, if I have been misinformed, darling, then I'll ask them to change your room. I know it's hard to believe, but this isn't meant to be a punishment. Perhaps a private . . ."

"No!" Dani shook her head and checked her voice level. "No, thank-you, mother. We really are fine now." She looked directly at her mother and was stunned at how little she was, Dani's height. She shrunk! When did that happen? "See, that first day Scratch made a lot of cracks because I wouldn't talk, but, see, I'm talking now, right? Right? Right?"

Her mother finally picked up on her cue and nodded vigorously.

"Anyway, she said—Scratch, I mean—said that I probably got off on getting smacked around. . . ."

Her mother flinched again and recovered more slowly this time.

"Anyway, anyway, I was pretty rotten to her, and she was kind of rotten to me. So we had a few words, or at least she did, and I sort of hauled up and slugged her." Dani caught her breath. "See?"

"Well," her mother tugged down her suit jacket, "there's a first time for everything, isn't there, dear?"

Whoa, where did that come from? Hey, was this going good now? Was anyone around to notice that it was going good, if it was going good, that is. Oops, pay attention, she's still talking to you, idiot, idiot, idiot.

". . . fortunate there's no long-term physical consequences. . . ."

Loser.

"We—I mean, I—researched this clinic to death, darling. And Dr. Thurber has such a brilliant reputation."

Death? Dead idiot.

". . . and you're so young yet. . . ."

Idiot cow!

Dani looked around for her father. Nope. Her mother seemed to be receding and advancing, mouthing words that Dani could barely hear. It must be close to meds, she thought. That's it! There, that felt good. She was delighted with herself for making such a coherent connection. It's probably the meds. Good girl.

She glanced at the lounge, catching Kevin's goofy, earnest smile and threw one back.

"Another friend, darling? That's wonderful. And . . . about your roommate, too. If you're happy—well, not happy, but satisfied—then I am, too. Your hair," her mother pointed at her own head, "your beautiful hair is growing back."

"Yeah, well," Dani ran her hands through it. "I don't know what I was . . . it was probably symbolic of something or other, eh?" Her mother couldn't seem to stop staring. She was looking at Dani like she had grown horns or something. What?

Mrs. Webster stepped forward again but then clearly thought better of it. She rummaged for her car keys instead. "Well, I'm sure your hairstyle is very MTV or this minute or whatever the word is for 'cool' these days." She smiled. "All right then, darling. They were adamant; they said just a couple of minutes this time. Just a glance, they said." Her mother bristled again or . . . was she trembling? How can you tell the difference? How in God's name are you supposed to know? Idiot.

"I don't want to risk . . . would Tuesday be okay? I'd come every single day, I have been, you know. But they say Tuesday is best, but I'll be here regardless, but Tuesday . . ."

Dani reached in and summoned a nod. "Tuesday? Tuesday is good." When was Tuesday? It sounded like a long time away. Relief swept over her; she was flooded with goodwill. "I like your lipstick, Mother. It matches that coral necklace really nice."

"Oh," her hand flew to her neck, "I always wear it. The necklace, always. Remember darling? You and Kelly bought it for me when you were little. It's so special. Honey, you were seven and

Kelly was four. I knew it was all your doing, and yet you let her give it, letting on that it was all her idea. By the end of the day, Kelly had us believing that she dove for the coral herself." Her mother looked as if someone had let the air out of her. "I always wear it, Dani." Her fingers fluttered nervously around the coral. "Always."

The peach pit of fear that had taken permanent residence in Dani's stomach awoke and roamed around. "Take care of her, Mother. Promise to take care of Kelly."

Sandra Webster crumbled. "Kelly? Oh Dani . . . oh . . ."

Panic crashed in on Dani in waves. She had done something wrong again. What? What? It was bad this time. Idiot. She was furious that she didn't know. She never knew. "I said . . ." She inhaled, counting out the beats, and exhaled. "Take care of Kelly! What's so wrong with that? With me gone, he's gonna lay into her! When are you going to get it? What has to happen? What!"

Kevin stuck his head around the post and was making chopping signs with his hand. Cut?

Her mother's arms reached out and then dropped. "I'm not supposed to burden you with anything. But Dani, you at least have to know this." Her hands flew around, she played with her finger, with an invisible ring.

No ring!

"Danielle, I've left your father. I left him the day after you were admitted. Do you understand? He won't hurt you or . . . or anyone again. I know you don't, can't trust me, but do believe this. I will keep him away from you. He can't come here. He can't even try to call you, or anything. It's a lot of legal stuff that you don't have to know or worry about, but I can promise, Dani. Never, never again." She repositioned her handbag. "There's lots and lots of things, darling. Changes, I mean. We'll have a lot to talk about when you're ready. But only when you're ready. Maybe . . . well, thank-you for seeing me. I know, well, I can imagine . . . I really can." She looked like someone had taken away all her toys. "Till Tuesday, darling."

Her mother turned and vanished. She was sucked out of the sliding doors.

Dani remained cemented to the linoleum tiles. Vanna White turned over five letter G's to the enthusiastic applause of Kevin, Bobby, and three boys she didn't know. She tried to remember how to breathe. She left him? In, two-three-four, out, two-three-four. Concentrate. But her thoughts refused to be collected. Kevin started toward her. Sentence fragments . . . *so Kelly was* . . . swirled like November leaves. She'd race, out of breath to retrieve one . . . *she left him* . . . only to have it crumble in her hands. It should've been, *We left him.*

Kevin reached her side just as Harold, looking completely ridiculous, rolled up with the meds trolley. He lurched for the clipboard with all the grace of a linebacker. "Kevin, you handsome bugger, you're off the afternoon dope entirely and, uh, Dani my little chatterbox." He searched around the little dixie cups. "Here's your poison. Sorry I'm late, kiddies. Hope nobody's seeing nothin' they shouldna' oughtta been seein'." He was having trouble finding the brake for the trolley. "Man, this sucks."

Dani was mesmerized by the way Harold's tattoos slithered when his muscles flexed and contracted.

"Yous all know I'm much better at the sensitive touchy-feely stuff, right?"

Dani smiled. At least on the inside she smiled. She wasn't a hundred percent sure what the outside was doing. She stared at the perfect arrangement of little flower dixie cups filled with pastel-colored pills.

"Drink up, kid," he touched her. His fingertips felt like warm sandpaper. She wanted to melt into them. "Come on, Dano," he winked. "It'll give ya big boobs."

She caught a glimpse of Scratch way down the hall.

"Hey, Scratch," Kevin yelled. "How's about joining Dani and me, and we'll go to the movies together?"

Scratch squinted, eyeing Dani, the dixie cup, and the meds trolley. "Sure." She trotted over. "Gulp it down, Sherlock. Time's a wasting."

Dani took the dixie cup and swallowed. She knew to swallow. She left him? Left him where? *I've left your . . . I, I, I . . .*

Harold rumbled off with his clipboards and trolley, cursing at the protesting wheels the whole time. Scratch stared at Dani. "Stay with us, Dani." She turned to Kevin accusingly. "What the hell happened?"

"I don't know." Kevin reddened so much his freckles disappeared. "It was going pretty good except for the bad bits."

"Morons! I'm surrounded by morons!" Scratch groaned. "Dani, keep it together. Remember all of Little Group is going to watch *Girl Interrupted* in . . ." she glanced at her watch ". . . five minutes ago. You remember Little Group, Thurber's merry band of privileged baby addicts and psychos?"

"Hey!" Kevin cuffed her.

"Sorry, and amiable fags."

Kevin looked like he had just won a prize, and he cuffed her again. Instead of blasting Kevin for touching her, Scratch continued to scan Dani. She moved closer and muttered, "If you're going to check out, do it during the film. Not now, not in here, got it?"

Check out? Dani felt like she could just float away, she was as light as a silk blouse.

Kevin also stepped closer to her. "Yeah, can you believe that Yolanda rented *Girl Interrupted?* I think she figures she's the heftier, smarter version of Whoopi Goldberg."

"Oh, sit on it," growled Scratch. "Anything's better than *Forrest Gump.* If I see that lame thing one more time, I'm going to fall on my sword."

"I thought they took all your swords away," said Kevin.

"Oh, ha-ha." She made violent gagging noises. "What do you think of the Whoopi versus Yolanda comparison, Dani. You're a big movie buff? At least, that's what someone wrote on your intake charts."

"She left my father."

"Yolanda?" Kevin was aghast. "Where?"

"Shut up," said Scratch.

"I think they're getting a divorce."

"Oh!" said Kevin. "Your parents. Great! Got it. That's great!"

"I hope she sucks him dry," offered Scratch. "Dani?"

"It's okay," nodded Dani. She nodded for quite some time. Finally, she turned to Kevin. "It's okay, I'm here. Thanks for watching out for me, Kevin."

Kevin was busy looking modest when Scratch smacked him. "Hey! I'm the one who made him!"

Dani smiled. "I know."

"We're off then." Kevin linked an arm through Dani's.

After a moment's hesitation, Scratch grimaced, made sure everyone noticed, then linked up on Kevin's other side. After some passionate bickering, they transformed the long commons corridor into a yellow brick road.

Scratch led off. "We-e-e're off to see the psychos, the wonderful psychos of Oz. We hear they are, really bizarre, the wonderful psychos of Oz."

They skipped by the lounge. The TV screen was now presided over by Alex Trebek. Only Bobby was left watching.

They skipped by Harold and his rickety trolley. Dani heard him complaining later that he couldn't get that stupid song out of his head for the rest of the day.

They skipped farther and farther down the corridor, farther and farther away from the pungent aroma of cinnamon that was coursing through the commons.

April 11

Dear Kelly,

Wow, I've been in here for two whole months!!! My, how time flies when you're not in touch with reality. Just kidding, I'm as sharp as a tampon. So you're not going to believe how crazed (ha, ha) I've been that you haven't written back to me when all the while you didn't even get my first letter. I've seen Mommy Dearest a couple of times and she explained it all. Sort of. You moved! Who knew? Too weird for words. Is it true? Did she really leave Daddy? How? Why? Never mind why—what I mean is, why now? Are you all right? Just where is this condo? No Daddy! Every time I think of it, I have to up my medication (kidding).

My shrink says that Mom's been going to a shrink (now, there's a family you can be proud of). Did you know she's been going to a shrink? Like, for a long while now too, plus she's seeing this Dr. Richardson here about me. When does she have the time to decorate anyone's faux library? By the way, how does it feel to be the only normal one?

I'd recreate my first letter for you except that I can't remember a single thing I said. Daddy's probably burned it by now. They have us hopping here. I just got out of this wonky math class. Yup, they make us go to classes. In theory it's so we don't fall too far behind. In reality it's all just one step up from basket weaving. Believe me, I know more French than the nervous little Arab who's our "teacher," and that's pretty pathetic since I've been flunking out the past three terms.

Anyway, anyway, I don't have time for a major update because I have to be in One on One (shrink talk) in a minute. Thing is, to get out of here you have to talk nonstop, emote all over the place, and "give it up," as they say in Little Group (later). It's, like, I know all that and I get it and everything, it's just that every time it's my moment to shine, my tongue gets velcroed to the roof of my mouth. Hard to believe, huh?

Thing is, last week in Little Group, I actually got into the Game a bit. Well, they were all over me. You don't mind, do you? Janice, this challenged Barbie doll, thinks I'm spinning some Harry Potter series and she's panting for the next six installments. Thing is, thing is . . . I'm a tad hazy on a couple of details. It must be the meds. I blame everything on the meds (hey, it works for me). Anyway, Scratch, my Gestapo roommate (see first letter, ha!), says I can't keep shrugging "I don't knows" if I ever want to be declared well or recovered or whatever they declare you when you're ready to blow this place.

Got it? I need some basic answers fast. I honestly can't remember a time when we weren't playing some version of the Game, can you? But Saraya and Yuras and that whole thing, that was like two years ago, right? Was it after I won All-County? And by the way, what do you remember about the last time, the last Game? Well, write absolutely the minute you get this and while you're at it tell me every single detail about the move, the new school, EVERYTHING. It's okay to write, don't be scared. I'll write a big letter as soon as I can. In the meantime don't worry, I'll be out of here in a minute, I can feel it.

Love (and I mean it)

Me

P.S. Don't tell anyone where I am, especially that hyena, Emily. She'll track you down and pretend she's all concerned. Next thing you know, she'll tell Megan and then it'll be out and I'm burnt toast at every private school in Westchester County. Tell her that Mom shipped me to Switzerland to help me get over the trauma of the divorce. HA!! I still have my touch.

P.P.S. Sorry about . . . well, where to begin, eh?

April 13

Dr. Thurber knocked over a heaping stack of files as he came around his desk to greet her. "Shoot. Come in, Dani. Sorry, I . . . uh . . . apologize for missing our last session—an emergency." He shoved papers randomly back into multicolored folders while waving her in. "Sit. Sit. You know the drill." He heaved the whole lot onto another teetering stack on the floor. Catching Dani's eye, he winked. "Don't worry, you're not in there. The color coding thing was Yolanda's attempt to organize me four years ago. You're in the computer. Everybody's in the computer." He went to retrieve his rickety, rolling chair. "It's just that I don't trust the darned computer."

Thurber's office seemed to get smaller every time Dani came in. She smiled at his chair. Scratch said that Yolanda had convinced Thurber that that chair was the only one in the entire clinic that could accommodate both his bulk and his bad back. As a result, they were inseparable. Clearly, even Thurber was afraid of Yolanda. At any given moment, you could see him rolling that stupid squealing chair from his office to Room 307 for Little Group or to the clinic boardroom and back. His stack of folders and clipboards hiccuped and lurched on the seat the whole way. There was a thriving staff numbers game based on successful chair trips per week. Dani, Kevin, and Scratch were lobbying Harold to get a piece of the action.

Dani settled into the down-filled wingchair. She couldn't remember how many times she'd been there; yet she was always surprised by how Thurber seemed to fill the whole office. Everything about him was foreign to her. Nothing ever matched, and his clothes looked like they'd gone straight from the dryer onto his back. Dani's world was populated by men like her father. There were no casual days in Mark Webster's universe. Lean, whippet bodies were swaddled in slate gray Italian suits and immaculate white shirts. Slender, antiseptic hands lied about their force.

Thurber's hands were the size of tractor tires. His index and middle fingers were still stained, though he insisted that he hadn't had a cigarette in weeks. He had chronic bed hair, even though he looked like he hadn't slept in days. The man was a mess. But then William Thurber would smile and look better than God. Everybody said so. This time, she looked right at him and offered up the best of her most sincere smiles.

He grinned back. "Well, good, we both seem to be pretty pleased with ourselves." He reached for the tape recorder and popped a piece of gum into his mouth. "Ready to rumble?"

Date: April 13
Time: 2:30 p.m.
Presiding Therapist: Dr. William Thurber
Patient: Danielle Webster
Transcript Code: 807-9

WT: Okay, Ms. Webster, you'll be relieved to know that there are no more photo albums, questionnaires, or associations. We're ready to move into the radical phase of your . . . ah . . . therapy—we're just going to talk. Are you up for that?

DW: Uh-hmm.

WT: You're looking better and better every time I see you. I don't know if you're noticing that, but it's apparent to everyone around here. Speaking up in Little Group was a real milestone, too. Psychiatrists love milestones. Do you feel up to talking a little bit more about your Game episodes?

DW: Uh-hmm.

WT: Good. Excellent. Well, then, let's see. . . . You've said it starts with a smell, right? Remember, I've explained that that's part of what's called a dissociative aura? I know knowing is important to you.

DW: Uh-hmm.

WT: Yes. Well. And the smell, it's always cinnamon, right?

(blank)

WT: A really strong cinnamon?

(blank)

WT: Uh, Dani? The smell?

DW: Uh-hmm, yeah. I'm trying, really. After the smell, the cinnamon, the air gets all powerful, like electricity, you know? It makes . . . makes everything wavy, like, like when you're driving on a really hot day and there are all these wavy puddles on the road and you think when you get there that there's going to be a splash, with the puddle, I mean. You're sort of a puddle right . . . right now . . . sort of . . . but in the actual Game, well, to tell you the truth I sort of forget some things, and, well, I've written to Kelly. . . . What?

WT: Nothing, Dani. Trust me, this isn't an exam. There are no right and wrong answers. It's okay to forget.

DW: Did you, like, forbid her to write me or something?

WT: I would never do that, Dani. I promise. Take some very deep breaths using your stomach muscles like we've been practicing. Relax. Breathe deep. Let the anxiety go, two-three-four. . . .

DW: I forget so much, you know? I hate that. I just hate it.

WT: Let it go, Dani. You're safe here. Let the fear go. Breathe in, two-three-four. Just let it go. You're safe. That's better, two-three-four. Much better. Dani? Dani . . .

The girls raced. Ran full throttle back to the blue grass. Dani's lungs burned as she whipped by scrub maple shoots. There it was, the first monster. Dani geared up and easily cleared a massive oak trunk. Except that in the Game, downed tree trunks were dangerous. Each one was really a dragon fitfully napping under a lazy sun. You had to clear their knobby spines just so . . . or . . . It hit her midflight. *Hey!* She landed and ran even faster. *It was good again.*

"Warrior Princesses!" roared Kelly, gallumphing three tree trunks back.

"Amazing Amazons!" called Dani, ripping over the next birch dragon. Kelly, master Amazon klutz, tripped over the oak dragon, requiring a full-pitched battle before the girls could call in a "vanquish victory." They fell in a heap over the destroyed carcass.

"Am I not stupendous, fellow warrior?"

"Yeah, you're a miracle in motion, all right," groaned Dani.

"I can do anything!" Kelly bowed toward her sister and then began fingering the tree trunk. "Da-da-da-da-da-da- . . . dum. De . . . da-da- . . . dum. De . . . da-da . . . dum."

Beethoven's "Für Elise." Kelly's recital piece. It had been Dani's recital piece.

"I will be exceptionally, especially, brilliant tonight. I will make you proud." Kelly posed for the cameras and bowed.

You'll make *him* proud, Dani winced.

"Da-da-da-da-da-da . . . dum."

Why did she have to pick the same darn piece? Dani began to sweat, the kind where it feels like you're sweating on the inside. Recital sweat.

"De . . . da-da- . . . dum."

Same darn piece.

Dani's last recital was almost two years ago to the day. She'd been sick all week with an ear infection. Her father thought she was faking it. So Dani started to fake feeling fine while swallowing handfuls of Tylenol. She had convinced herself that she was fine. She was fine when she got on stage. She was fine right up until she took her introductory bow, and then it felt like her head was going to fall off and roll down the aisle. Still, she had entered the first movement breathing into it with perfect rhythm. Dani's whole body knew "Für Elise" like a prayer. She had played it, paced it, eaten it, and dreamed it for months. Finally, she would do a good thing. She could, she would, this night, make him proud. He would stand up and clap for her. The pounding in her ear was worse. The last few Tylenols had worn off by Jessica Rupert's solo. The infection burned in and around her ears, her right eye.

Doesn't matter. Concentrate! Smarten up. Dani strained to hear. She couldn't. She strained to feel.

"De . . . da-da- . . . dum."

He was out there in the dark. Waiting for her to stumble. Still, she almost danced through the second movement. Good. Listen. Listen. She was hearing all the wrong things—coughing, chairs scraping. Her heart was going to burst out of her chest. Listen! Just as she entered the third movement. No-o-o. Her fingers blurred. No-o-o. They bled into each other. No.

A sympathetic gush of "o-o-o-h-h-hs" escaped from the velvet darkness of the auditorium. Dani stopped. She knew what she had to do. Just like William Marcuso, two years ago. You had to go back to the very beginning. "Inhale deeply," Miss Eberly would've said. "Then exhale very, very slowly. Take your time." The competing fragrances from all the jewelled moms fought for attention. His glare sliced through the Chanel No. 5 and L'Air du Temps.

Hands up.

"Da-da-da-da-da-da- . . . dum."

Sweat or no sweat, she was pure and strong. Controlled all through the first two movements. Speeding lightly into the third. *Good. So good. Ah-h-h . . .*

"De . . . de . . . de . . ."

No. Too fast. Too fast. Too . . .

Her thumbs crossed, pretzeled.

Stupid. Oh God, so stupid.

Again Dani stopped. Out there, the audience felt like a blanket, thick with woolly concern. She could imagine all the "What's with the Webster child?" whispers. She was sick with the strain of listening through the crashing in her ears. She was sick with shame. Back to the beginning.

Hands up.

"Da-da-da-da-da-da . . ."

I know it. I don't have to hear it. I know it. I'll get it.

"De . . . da-da- . . . dum."

Her hands were wet.

Where does all that sweat come from?

Sliding.

Loser sweat.

She didn't even finish the second movement.

Pained groans. It was so hot, wavy, like in the car on the way over. Dani felt Miss Eberly's heels, click, click, clicking down the marble aisle, sheet music in hand.

No.

She wiped her hands on her skirt.

No more.

Rather than wait for Miss Eberly and the music, Dani shot up, fists clenched. The bench screamed at the floor in protest. She turned to the audience. "Uh . . . please forgive me, I'm so sorry." Her voice reached out to the darkness. Dani bowed and strode off stage.

The applause was thunderous and good-natured.

Mr. Webster clapped louder than anyone.

"Promise?" Kelly's whine pierced the nightmare. "Promise you'll sit near the front?"

Dani nodded.

The crush after the performance was maddening. Kelly clung to her like a suction cup while Mrs. Webster kept smoothing out her linen skirt and smiled sweetly at the other moms. Her mother had joined them at the conservatory. She had come late. It was "a very important meeting, darling." Too late. Murmuring that it was way past Kelly's bedtime, her mother and sister vanished after Kelly's third cookie. Dani and her father were left marooned in a sea of tinkling pink punch and sympathy.

There was an ocean in her head. Hot, furious waves crashed

against her ear. She had done it in the end, defied him. No doubt about it. Too late now. Good for me.

It was like that.

A wave rolled in and she was invincible.

The wave rolled out and she was terrified.

A sea of people kept coming up to them. They always came to him no matter where they were. They fawned over him. They wanted to be near Mark Webster, wanted to make Mark Webster smile. He placed a perfect pinstriped arm around her shoulder.

It felt like she was carrying the piano.

They both weathered indulgent "You'll nail it next year, kid," and "Nice of you to give someone else a chance at All-County." Mr. Webster alternately chuckled and shrugged. Miss Eberly was tracking them from across the room. Her face shadowed between concern for Dani and glowing bursts of congratulations offered to her favorites. Mr. Webster caught her eye, winked, and waved her off. He patted Mr. Rupert on the shoulder and added a "Look out, Juilliard," for Jessica. Jessica beamed at him. You'd think he'd given her a new bike. After forever, they left.

The Mercedes clicked shut like a compression chamber. The silence in that car was the loudest sound that Dani had ever heard.

He didn't even raise his voice. Actually, he didn't say anything. He didn't need to.

Dani wasn't buckled. She was fiddling with her shoelace.

The blow, when it came, threw her head over into the car door.

Her ear smashed into the beautifully crafted door handle.

Something inside of her burst and oozed, made a mess. She was always making a mess.

". . . and promise you'll wave. I'm going to wear your black velvet, but Mom and me have to be there way early, remember?" Kelly's fingers still played, but in midair now and mercifully silent. "You and Daddy have to get there early, too, right? To be at the front, right? To wave. So I know. Promise?"

Never again. Dani stood up and threw her arms around Kelly. She kissed the top of her warm, sunny head. She had to stand on her tiptoes to do it. Kelly hugged back. Nobody hugged like Kelly. "I promise that you will be brilliant and I will be shining under your brilliance. But we better hustle back right now or we'll both be brilliant dog dirt."

"Okay." Kelly skipped ahead, delighted with herself.

Dani's stomach turned over. "Hey, Kelly." Her sister almost slid over on the mossy path. "And next time, I promise for sure, we'll do the binding ceremony. The whole 'Lavender's Blue' song with every single verse and everything. Okay?"

"Yeah?"

"Absolutely."

(blank)

WT: You've come out of it now. I can tell and I know you can tell. What just happened, I believe, was a dissociative episode. That's twice with me. You were very relaxed, almost in a hypnotic state, highly suggestible, understand? You're nodding, that's good.

(blank)

WT: Would you like to talk about it? Talking about it can help to make the whole experience less alarming.

(blank)

WT: Were you in the Game, Dani?

(blank)

WT: It's all right, Dani, there is nothing to be frightened of. Nothing bad will happen. You have my word on it. It's okay. To tell you the truth, I'm glad you're nodding at me. I won't push. You are doing so well. I know it's frustrating, but you really are doing so well. The episodes are thinning. You're making important connections to people, your friends, Little Group, and even your mother. We'll end now, but I want you to be clear about how much progress you've been making, okay?

(blank)

WT: We'll do even better next time.

DW: Dr. Thurber?

WT: Yes, Dani?

DW: Thanks.

END OF SESSION: 3:30 P.M.

April 16

Dani didn't want to go to the Career Day Lecture. She wasn't sure of much, but she was sure she didn't want to grow up to be an assistant television producer. Their entire wing was quiet. The way the bottom of a swimming pool is quiet. She'd been staring at the writing paper for almost an hour, held at ransom by the black and white line drawing of Pooh and his honey pot on the top right-hand corner of the sheet. It was Scratch's writing paper. "Go figure," she sighed and finally picked up the pen.

Dear Kelly,

Hi, it's me again! How are ya? Actually where are you??? I don't mean exactly. Like I said, I know all about the move, the separation, new condo etc., etc., etc. On my better days I can remember all the changes and even the sequence they all occurred in. Haaa, kidding!!! What I mean is, how come you haven't come? What's a big sister to think?

Mom's been a thousand times. She kept coming even

when I wouldn't see her and she would just wait and wait for the entire visiting period. It was embarrassing. Anyway, she was making the rest of the inmates restless so they forced me to see her (sort of kidding).

I bet even Daddy has tried to come, not that they'd let him anywhere near me. The place does have its advantages, you know. Hey, someone socked it to him and he's footing the bill for all of this (Scratch still passes time by hacking into the daily entry logs). I even asked the all-powerful Yolanda about whether you're allowed to come or what. Like Mom, she just short of shuts down whenever I ask about you. I'm beginning to suspect a conspiracy. In fact, I'd consider being paranoid but the medication keeps kicking in. Haa!

I know all this is a mess for you. There are entire minutes when I'm not totally preoccupied with myself and I remember to obsess about you. Did he go after you too? Is that it? Is that what finally jolted Mother, why she's pretending? If he touched you I'll kill him. Hey, what can they do—stuff me in a loony bin?

It's like a nonstop happening in here, meals, snacks, crafts, lectures, classes, one-on-one sessions, family therapy sessions, Little Group sessions, C Ward meetings, awkward visits with family etc., etc., etc. It could be worse, way worse. Little Group is just like it sounds and it's pretty okay. Except (and this is a major exception) for Jared who is a deviant rapist pod-person. Kevin thinks that Jared can't get turned on unless he's hurting someone and I believe it. Thing is that leaves me all confused about Janice, his current love slave (yup, apparently there were others). I'd like to hate her but now I have to feel sorry for her or else what kind of person would that make me?

Then there's William, obsessive-compulsive (you know, counts a lot and washes so much his hands are always bleeding). Bobby is a sweet little guy but we don't really know what his thing is since he hardly says boo. Agnes is a low-level crying bulimic (ambitious type A anorexics are on D Ward and serious criers i.e., manic depressives, are over there with them). There's also Sam who sometimes thinks he's Jimi Hendrix and sometimes Doris Day. We like Doris better cause she has great stories about the old studio system in its glory days and Jimi is a moody SOB. Then there's Kevin who's a peach and my friend (gender identity disorder—don't ask, I don't think it exists). And I already told you about Scratch who should be running this place. Come to think of it, she is. I'm proud and stunned to say she's also my best friend.

Most of the kids outside of C Ward are absolutely snake-pit material. Don't let anyone tell you that you can't judge a book by its cover.

Another thing is that they still electroshock people. Voluntarily. Can you believe it?!!! How nuts is that? Good morning, I'd like to sign up for a brain fry right after tie-dying at ten o'clock! Scratch said that she thought about it once. Like Kevin, she's been to a whole lot of other places. Anyway, Kevin talked her out of it and they've been joined at the hip ever since. Well, that and they're both too tidy for words!

If you think I was bad for not seeing Mother for a few weeks, there's this multiple on D Ward with eleven different personalities and none of them will have anything to do with her mother. I admire a lunatic with principles. Anyway, Mother and I do the visit thing now, and we do the family therapy thing, and like WHAT IS IT WITH HER??? Nobody changes that much. Thurber says we have both endured an environment (i.e., Daddy) that helped precipitate a "disconnect" in our lives. I volunteered that mine was the Game because page 367 of my trusty Mental Manual pretty well lays it all out, and I thought I'd get brownie points for acknowledging it (I did).

How DID you stay so sweet and sane?

Did you catch the bit where I mentioned that I have friends. Real friends, Kelly, not fake friends like those leeches Emily and Megan. Too cool for words? Remember this, Kelly, all you get from the cool kids is freezer burn. Got it? Okay, that's the sermon for the decade. Anyway, I'm just me with them, whatever "me" is at the moment. The stupendous thing is . . . they won't dump me when they "know" because they "know" already. You'll love them. I told them all about you.

I'm getting better Kelly. I'm still not sure from what exactly but maybe when I'm all better I'll know. So you shouldn't be afraid of saying or doing the wrong thing if you come. Is that it? Don't be afraid. It's a waste. Besides, I've got the fear thing covered for the entire planet. So don't worry, just come. Or you could call (914-555-1289) from 7:30 to 10:30 on weeknights and it's wide open on weekends. Yeah, call. I'd do just about anything to hear your voice. People call all the time or write or just turn up, you know?

I WILL make you proud of me again.

All my good love,
Dani

Dani numbered the pages, lined them up, and hugged the sheets close. After a time, she folded the letter, carefully lining up the edges. Then, rather than putting it in the envelope on the dresser, Dani got up and tucked the pages into her back pocket. She turned off the light, smiled at the dark room, and ran off to catch what was left of how to become a barracuda.

April 20

Dani fanned her freshly painted fingernails while Kevin paced. He groaned dramatically each time he rounded their armchair.

Kevin hated being late. "Where is she already? Little Group starts in exactly . . ." He examined his watch as if he didn't know down to the second what time it was. ". . . four minutes. You know, that polish might look just a tad better if you didn't bite your nails to bloody little nubs."

"Yeah, well," Dani shrugged, "Scratch says we all got to start somewhere. Maybe instead of Be-Bop Blue I should've gone for Silver Screech?"

"I don't believe this." He glared at his watch. "Where is she?"

"Will you relax?"

"Did she go to the tree?"

Dani stopped fanning. "What tree?"

He shrugged and checked his watch at the same time. "We found this amazing old oak in the back forty last week. It's the size of a house. It's got really cool vibes, you know? We've decided to use it as our office."

"Oh," Dani whispered. What did you expect, idiot? Idiot. Idiot. Idiot.

"She said that you're going to love it."

"Me? She did!?"

"Well, actually, she said it's going to remind you of your 'stupid ravine thing.'"

Dani grinned at her fingernails. "I love Be-Bop Blue. Don't worry, Kev, I think she said something about a phone call."

"Oh now, you do have me panicked." Kevin folded himself into the chair. "You know very well that no one phones Scratch. No one in her family, thank God, I may add. Her friends gave up, like, two institutions ago. Hmmm, her old headmaster calls from time to time."

"No. It was some friend of her dad's. I thought you knew."

"Which dad? The current one, the stepdad she sort of liked, not the—"

"Her real dad, Kevin, the dead one. It was some dermatologist or gynecologist or something."

"Oh!" Kevin brightened. "Dr. Steve. Yeah, okay. He's cool. Yeah," Kevin loosened up, "that's good. He was best friends with Mr. McKenzie, and he's been trying to . . . well, at least he calls and he's even come a few times, you know?" Kevin jumped up and popped himself on the window ledge, knocking over most of Scratch's lotions in the process.

"Kevin!" Scratch burst in. "Get your ass off my Aqua! That's an entirely new line from Sephora! Let's move, kiddos. Do you know how late we are? Thurber's going to grind us!"

"Sorry."

"So sorry."

"Sorry."

Everyone was already in place when the trio tripped through the door. Dr. Thurber looked up at the wall clock and grimaced. "I'm going to have to note it, guys."

Ever since Dani's encounter with Jared, they always sat together. Dani in the middle with Scratch and Kevin on either side protecting her flank, but this time there were only two free seats together. Scratch curled her lip at Lucy, a relatively new depressive who immediately scuttled off to sit with Janice and Jared. Thurber pretended not to notice.

"Okay, thank-you, Janice." Thurber took a sip of his coffee. "Anyone else with a memory that they now feel is questionable or at least open to interpretation?"

"I do," said Dani stunned to hear her own voice chirp up.

No one moved.

"I mean, I remember more stuff about the Game."

Scratch turned to her bug-eyed.

"I think."

Kevin considered his top-siders.

"Yeah, uh-huh, it comes to me sort of like in a video."

Jared threw her a little kiss from across the room. "Well, whoop-dee-doo, the Ice Queen is deigning to share another fractured fragment with the rest of us plebes." Jared's Georgia drawl turned "Ice Queen" into "Ass Ko-o-w-e-e-n."

Scratch was out of her chair like a bullet.

"Shut up, you southern-fried piece of . . ."

"That's enough. Both of you." Thurber's voice didn't break. He continued to hold Dani's gaze as he addressed Jared and Scratch. "Check your language, check your intentions, or leave. Dani, why don't you take us there."

Out of habit Dani searched the bank of windows behind Thurber for inspiration. But it was too cloudy. The blind wasn't asking for assistance today.

Thurber cleared his throat indelicately and took another swig. "Dani?"

"Right." Dani closed her eyes, commanding the images to come. "Right." She opened her eyes and scanned the circle. Everyone, except Jared of course, looked . . . what, eager? "Where were we . . . wait, I remember." She hugged herself with relief. "It was still early afternoon, but I'd pretty well convinced Kelly that we couldn't do a full Game. That involved a lot of rituals, sacred this and sacred that. Then there's the divining for signs and clues, and sometimes, but not always, Yuras actually puts in an appearance, you know? Anyway, full Game is, like, seriously time-consuming and involved. We really didn't know where Saraya was imprisoned after all."

Everyone nodded earnestly, pretending to remember what she was talking about.

"What I mean is . . . we were a very long way off from freeing Saraya, let alone vanquishing Yuras." The words tumbled out. What had she been afraid of? This was easy. "I mean, I wanted to and everything, but Kelly had this big recital that night and we had to get home to get cleaned up and everything. I mean, we just really had to go, right? "

She looked to Thurber, whose finger was tracing the outline of his coffee mug. Did he look pleased? Sure, why wouldn't he?

"But Kelly . . . well, she wheedled out a stopover at the Sacred Stream, which is on the way back. Sort of. Anyway, I agreed to just a few minutes. No ceremony or blessings or major Game stuff. So we raced there. We raced everywhere, you know, all the time. Kelly's as big as me, bigger now maybe, but nowhere near as fast. It's like one of the few things I know how to do, be fast, I mean. We loved to race."

Dani had stopped checking around for reactions.

She was running.

She ran like the wind. In fact, Dani lost her bluegrass headband to the wind, but she reached the bank miles ahead of Kelly.

"The winner of the world and champion of the universe, Danielle Webster! Tenga verimuch. Tenga." Dani swaggered and swiveled, acknowledging her fans. A bank of scrub lilacs swayed enthusiastically.

"Okay, okay," groaned Kelly. "Elvis can leave the building now."

"As always, a gracious loser."

They veered into the willows that protected the embankment. "It's running!" Kelly hopped about clapping her hands. "The stream's still there. I can hear it!"

"Brilliant hearing . . . guess that's why you're captain." Dani plopped down and whipped off her shoes and socks. "Okay then, let's get purified."

They took off their pouch packs and trod gingerly through the curtain of willow branches that hid the entrance to the stream—

"o-e-o-oing" and "ow-w-ing" over every piercing twig and pebble.

Dani squelched into the cold, oozing earth first. The mud sucked at her toes. Kelly followed, whistling and making no effort to roll up her jeans. After the initial searing shot of pain which bolted from her feet to her forehead, Dani's legs would numb up nicely. "Ah-h-h-h . . ." Numb and pure—purified. She had to wait until Kelly turned purple. That was Kelly's sign of purification.

"Am I purple yet?" Kelly was shivering violently.

"Grape jelly."

"Thank God, I'm starving."

"Me, too."

They clambered out of the rushing water.

The girls found a perfect spot under the arch of the biggest willow canopy. They stretched themselves out onto a patch of furry, spring crabgrass and began the process of settling into each other. Legs flat and back to back. This took time. You had to position your butt, the small of your back, your head, and especially your shoulder blades just so, or they'd slice into the other person. Done properly, weighted just right, it was better than a bean bag chair.

"Okay?" called Kelly.

"Perfect."

"What do you got?"

Dani surveyed her treasure. "One package of melting Maltesers."

"Outstanding. Divide them properly, no cheating with counting two that are glued together as one."

Dani ignored her. "And three triangles of that weirdo cheese that's wrapped in the tin foil with the cow on the front."

"You're losing your touch, Dani. I have here three, count 'em, three, packages of Rainbow Skittles to be washed down by . . . *ta-da!* . . . a family-size package of Snickers."

"Brilliant foraging, Captain." They smiled and they both knew they were both smiling.

"Tell me about Yuras." Kelly whipped around on her knees, causing Dani to plonk down hard on the grass.

"Ow! No!" Dani got up slowly.

"Please. Puleeze. Please."

"Stop, you're making me puke with all your whining."

"Okay, sorry." She placed her fingers on her forehead. "It's just that I'm not seeing him clear enough. We're not coming tomorrow, and we didn't actually play it today. I won't ask for anything else."

Dani groaned, defeated. She glanced back at the muddy, gurgling stream, looking for . . . she didn't know what for. "Yuras. Yuras is the personification of evil. Yet, he is so beautiful you could scarce behold him."

"I love that part."

"He never strides or stumbles. Yuras floats, though never leaves the ground. His body is bathed in diaphanous robes, and whenever he moves or gestures, the robes change hue, from pearlized clouds to iridescent blues."

"As soon as I get home, I'm looking those words up." Kelly made the same vow every time.

"And it is always misting around him, tiny drops of fine spray that also change color like a kaleidoscope of confetti. Oh, and Yuras has no hair anywhere on his person—yet you would never think that odd."

Kelly nodded gravely. "I know just exactly what you mean."

"But his eyes . . ."

"Yes?"

"That is where the evil presents itself. His eyes are such an endless black that they appear hollow. They are never-ending tunnels that lead to nothing. That is why he is so evil, Kelly. It is not possible to redeem Yuras. Yuras must be vanquished because he has no soul. Yuras must be vanquished before we can find true life."

Dani exhaled so slowly she thought she was going to float away. She surveyed the circle. Jared was doing that thing with his tongue, but the rest were rapt. She had done it. Gone and come back at will. Good, plain, memory.

"Yeah? So what happens, huh?" demanded Janice. "That's it? Do you win or what?"

"We didn't play that day. Remember?" Dani crossed and uncrossed her legs. "We just hustled on back home."

Janice looked crestfallen. "What a gyp!"

A couple of others nodded in agreement.

Dani wasn't prepared for that. "Well, see, that last Game, well, it was harder to . . . make it all happen."

"What do you mean, like a lie?" Janice looked panicky. "What happens to the Sarah chick. Do you free her or is that, like, next time?"

To his credit Jared looked disgusted.

"Saraya. The Goddess's name is . . . was . . . Saraya."

Bobby nodded thoughtfully. Bobby rarely spoke, but he could

always be counted on for sincere nodding.

"Okay." Janice was clearly annoyed. "So the next time, so you do whatever voodoo stuff you have to do and rescue the Sara chick and click off the bald guy, right?"

Dani wondered if Janice was on something she shouldn't be. "No-o-o-o . . . the point is that we didn't go again."

"You left her just hanging? Why?"

"I don't know." And she didn't. Dani curled up into herself holding on to her toes. She always remembered everything that had to do with the Game. Where did it go? She stared right through Janice. "Things happen, you lose interest. I don't know, maybe I started drinking then."

That shut her up.

Dani folded her arms across her chest. "It just felt . . ." she shrugged, "I wasn't into it as much. It happens," she shrugged. "One minute you're the master of all the magic in the universe, the whole kingdom of the Game, it's at your fingertips—and the next, it's gone. Poof."

Kevin and Bobby looked like they were going to cry.

Jared nudged Janice. "Oh look, Dr. Thurber," she pointed to the clock. "Lunch has started already and everything."

Thurber seemed to rouse himself from a reverie. "My, yes, well, excellent session." He had to shout above the chairs scraping and bodies flinging themselves out at top speed. "The canvas and methods we protect and amuse ourselves with as children could be important for all of us to explore." Bodies flew out the door. "Let's all think about that," he shouted, "for the next group."

Kevin slapped Dani on the back. Scratch rolled her eyes.

She did it.

She had made them understand. She had it all under control now. She could fill in the blanks any which way and they bought it. Man, she was good.

April 22

Jared was even uglier than usual that whole morning. Dani didn't have to look at him. She knew how this sort of thing went down and she was on hyper-alert. She could smell it off him in Little Group. Anyone caught in Jared's flight path today would be considered fair game. To top it all off, Kevin and Scratch had taken off somewhere right after lunch. Dani holed up in her room nursing a grudge about being left out. She would have stayed there brooding all afternoon, but she had to go to French. You got big points deducted for missing classes, no matter how useless they were.

Dani heard rather than saw Jared when she got up to the fourth floor. He was walking behind her. How far? She picked up her pace. She had just turned the west corner when she heard him kick open Janice's door.

"Yo baby! Come here, bitch."

A picture of Janice asking about the Game burned her for a nano-second. Dani pushed it aside and took off, sweeping through the meandering corridors at warp speed. She reached Room 522 stomach clenched, heart pounding, and in record time.

"One-forty-five, oh man!" Dani glared at the empty room. It always seemed that the earlier she got to class, the later good old Monsieur Aboud would make it. Monsieur was directionally challenged. Every successful trip up to the little room at the top of the clinic represented at least two abject failures requiring an orderly depositing him in the nearest corridor. French class had, by and large, stayed a private affair. Anyone else who had tried it was quickly put off by the round little teacher and never stayed more than two or three sessions.

Monsieur was Arab or Egyptian or something else that was equally exotic for Rockland County. Monsieur insisted that he spoke fifteen different languages. Unfortunately, English and French ranked somewhere near the bottom of the list. Scratch thought he was sweaty. Kevin thought he was just nervous. But that was okay with Dani. All of it. So she stayed, by herself.

She didn't want to hurt his feelings.

Groaning dramatically for the benefit of no one, Dani dragged herself over to the far window well that overlooked the clinic's parking lot. She settled in for her regular entertainment of matching the vehicle to the appropriate parent or staff. Staff generally favored sensible cars, with Tauruses and Honda Civics as the big winners. Thurber tooled around in a seven-year-old Volvo station wagon, while Yolanda had just bought a brand new used Toyota Corolla.

The parents, of course, were another story.

Today there were two, count 'em two, Hummers out there. Like what for, just in case they had to invade Scarsdale? There were also three BMWs, a Merc and a champagne-colored Jag that looked just like . . . her eyes swept back to the footpath, then back to the Jag, then back to the . . .

She saw him.

They told her over and over again: no way could he come here, see her. They said that, no way. Dani stopped breathing.

He was leaving.

"Wait." She whispered to the glass.

Was it him? She sidled up closer to the windowpane, framing her eyes against the sun. That stride, shoulders razor-sharp and straight. That stride, that Master of the Universe stride. She could feel the cashmere kiss of his suit from five floors up.

"Daddy."

He stopped.

Dani tried exhaling like they had been teaching her to, expelling it all, two-three, inhaling deep into the gut, four-five-six.

He turned. As he was turning he took off his suit jacket and draped it over his left arm. But he didn't walk back into the clinic. Mark Webster just stood there, looking . . . small. He was standing weird, too. His West Point posture seemed to be shrinking into itself. Something was wrong . . . off. She wanted to run away, call Harold, find Scratch.

He looked up!

Dani almost fell off the ledge. Reason wrestled with panic as she tried to absorb herself into the window well. No way could he see in. The interior on a sunny day read as black. She knew this from when she and Kevin tried to figure out where their rooms were. That was it! Daddy was counting off floors and windows, looking . . . oh God, he was looking for her room!

He got even smaller when he found it. He stared squinting against the sun searching. Then he rubbed his face; the gold of his wedding band caught the light and flickered at her like a code.

"Daddy."

Did he come for her? Did he try to see her? Did he . . . she watched him turn and walk away.

"Daddy . . . wait."

Dani tracked him like a laser all the way to the parking lot. Once there, he pulled on his jacket again and strode the rest of the way, filling the jacket, growing taller, more defined, harder, with every step.

The Jag roared to life, chewing through the silence around it.

The suit was like armor. She slumped against the window and clamped her eyes against threatening tears.

"Nice suit."

April 26

"Protection money?" Dani asked. "Protection from what?"

"What do you think?" Scratch shrugged. "It's just the boys so far."

Dani nudged her head toward Kevin, who was deeply engrossed in his lunch selection.

"Naw," Scratch shook her head. "Jared either doesn't consider Kev to be a boy, or he's saving him for something else."

Dani shivered. "Is there anything we can do?"

"Sure," Scratch stretched herself out. "It's clear that I'm going to have to kill him. I suppose, however . . ." she leaned in on Kevin, who was meticulously picking out the kidney beans from his beef burrito ". . . that a cold-blooded killing would play havoc with my release date, don't ya think?" She flung a fry at him.

"Who? What? What did I do now?"

"She's planning to 'off' Jared," said Dani.

They were at "their" table, a defiant Formica relic that had somehow escaped the renovation inflicted on the rest of the cafeteria over the past few months. Everywhere else, earthy, sage-green tables and chairs contrasted prettily with sunny walls dressed in Impressionist posters from the Met. Everyone knew it was their table.

It was just like at school really. The table closest to the food line was populated by Jared, Janice, and at least five other kids whom Scratch dismissed as Junior League juvenile delinquents. The table nearest the wall seemed to be reserved for kids who had food issues. They not only had to eat in the presence of a nurse, but had to write down what they were eating and how they felt about each bite. As a result, they looked like the clinic geeks. Then, although he was occasionally allowed to eat with them, Bobby usually joined the rest of Thurber's Little Group, which represented the clinic's swing group, or "wannabes." Kids from the other wards, whom Dani still couldn't identify, were scattered throughout the rest of the cafeteria. They were the loners.

Scratch had always hated the renovation, but today she seemed to take it personally. "Whose chain do they think they're yanking?" she yelled out to Yolanda, who was strolling by. "Hey, Yo. What is it with this reno? Institution by Disney? Do they figure we're all going to think we're in Provence instead of lockup?"

Yolanda rested her loaded tray on their table and surveyed the room critically. Dani was impressed by her selection. Green salad, no dressing, low-fat yogurt, an apple, and a double portion of fries with gravy and melted cheese. What was the thinking here?

"Now, honey," Yolanda crooned, "you know this is the sort of thing that keeps the mommies and daddies happy. Besides," she flashed a smile exposing her killer dimples, "we're going to up everyone's dosage, and, honey, you're all for sure going to think you're in the south of France."

"But not us, right, Yo?" the three of them chimed right on cue.

"Course not, children. Aren't you my favorites?" On that, Yolanda picked up her tray and sashayed over to her designated loner of the day.

"Where were we?" asked Kevin. "Oh yeah, well, I say piss on your release date. You go right ahead and kill Jared and to hell with the consequences." This was greeted with another fry.

Dani basked in the rhythmic patter of her friends' bickering. Friends? When did that happen? Friends? Yeah, it felt right, clean. "Well, I think he's nothing but bad news, all right."

Scratch beamed her a "well duh," look. "Dani darling, as much as I revel in all your little milestones, and Lord knows, it seems we're having one a minute lately . . ."

"Oh shut up, Scratch," said Kevin.

"Alison. I have decided that I want to be called Alison again. Dani's not the only one with milestones, you know. I plan to have one a day until I leave."

Kevin sighed dramatically. "Not everything is about you, you know."

"Since when?"

Dani and Kevin made retching noises.

"Oh, take a Valium. Dani, if you want a major milestone experience, how about taking a shower?"

"Scratch!" Dani tried to look injured.

"That's Alison to you, too. Besides, what are friends for?"

Dani grabbed a handful of her T-shirt and inhaled. "Okay, maybe I'm a teeny bit ripe. Actually, when was the last time I had a bath?"

"I force marched you into the shower a few days ago. Remember, Sherlock? It was after your one-on-one."

Dani rummaged around for the memory and came up empty. She smiled and nodded at Scratch.

"You do *not* remember, you little hosebag. I'm not Thurber. I can tell when you're deking me out."

"Scratch!" Kevin groaned.

"That's Alison! I'm going to have to write a memo about the name change thing, I can see it now."

Dani was still scanning for the shower memory when Jared morphed out of nowhere and loomed over them.

"O-o-o-ow goody, a group grope—two dykes and a queer. One of my favorite scenes."

"Hey, toad turd," Scratch spat. "My personal pathology is incest. You know, the thing you must be a product of. Then again," she paused for effect, "incest has six letters, such a big word for someone with such a little dick."

Jared gripped the table, raising it slightly. Janice was waving furiously to him at the far end of the cafeteria. She was pretty well popping out of her tube top with the exertion. He ignored her and continued clutching the table. The veins in his hands were raised and angry. Then, just as quickly as he'd appeared, he let go. Dani's mouth went dry. Before she could duck, he ran his fingers through her hair. His touch was repulsive. Intimate. She couldn't look away. Jared's eyes were watery and empty. Nobody was in there.

Scratch grabbed his hand in midair. "Time to crawl back into your cesspool."

Neither of them moved.

"Yolanda's in here, butt brain, and I can hear your buddies in F Ward calling out your name. They miss you, baby."

Jared tsk-tsked. "Premenstrual, darling, or did they take away your self-mutilation kit?"

Dani stood up. "You're oozing on our table." Now they had everyone's attention. The servers stopped serving. Not a single fork moved. "Get lost, Jared."

Jared clenched his jaw and turned to Kevin. Finally, after directing a few wet kisses at him, Jared swaggered over to Janice's table, which was already overflowing with the clinic's finest.

"Atta go, warrior princess baby!" whooped Scratch. "I think he likes you, Kevin."

All of Kevin's freckles dissolved into a furious mask.

"It's no joke," said Dani sitting down again. "He's just messed up enough that . . ." She stared at his table. "Who are all those kids? I don't recognize most of them."

Kevin began listing their transgressions. "Let's see—drug dealers, molesters, perverts . . ."

"Hey, Bible boy!" snapped Scratch. "This is my turf. They'd all be in prison if it weren't for daddy's dollars. Every last one of them is a serial killer in the making, including that slut with the thunder thighs, Janice. On paper, Jared's the cleanest . . . but I'll tell you now, that boy is on something. I don't know how he's doing it in here, but he's using."

"That's enough. Let's get out of here." Kevin got up. "Let's go to the tree."

Just like that. Nothing special. It was just assumed that she was included.

"You're on Grounds Pass, aren't you?" Kevin asked.

Dani nodded. She had been for over a month, but tried to avoid the outside. There were three kinds of passes at Riverwood—Internal, building only; Quad, courtyard only; and Full Grounds. Dani had trouble getting herself past the Quad. The Quad was always crammed with Quad types: mumblers and pacers who spent hours going back and forth or around and around, miraculously avoiding each other. They spooked her.

"Come on." Kevin pulled Dani to her feet.

The three of them marched out of the cafeteria, through the commons corridor, saluting Yolanda, and through three sets of sliding glass doors that magically sucked open and shut when they called out their pass numbers. Dani inhaled as they passed the perfect pacers and charged on through to Philosophers' Walk, which Scratch had rechristened Looney's Lane. Dani had to squint, even though it was a dull and heavy afternoon.

"It's going to rain," she said.

"Such a genius!" Scratch addressed the trees. "Tell me, was it the dark storm clouds that gave it away?"

Dani giggled. "No, it's just my heightened sense of reality. Must be yet another milestone."

Scratch rewarded her with a good shove. "Did you all see that? I'm beginning to reap the rewards of healthy human physical contact."

Dani and Kevin groaned in well-timed unison.

They passed dozens of ancient oaks, any of which could have been The Tree. "Hey," Dani finally asked, "what is it with you and this stupid tree? Why are we out here in the wilderness, for Godsake?"

"It has great karma." Scratch finally came to stop against a particularly gnarled giant. "And great privacy."

Kevin patted the trunk affectionately, then nodded to Scratch. "Now?"

Dani's stomach turned over. "What? What's going on?"

"Look, Dani." Scratch positioned herself just so on an exposed root. Kevin and Dani dropped down beside her. "I've been ready to leave for a while now. Thurber, Yo, even Richardson, they're kind of looking the other way when it comes to me, you know?"

Dani didn't.

"Thurber's okay, Dani, for a shrink I mean. Anywhere else, they'd scotch-tape me up and send me right back into the loving arms of my stepdaddy." She closed her eyes for a few seconds, then opened them, looking at Dani like she was searching for something. "Don't look all indignant. It's happened. My mother needs to believe my stepfather. Ipso facto, I got to stay away. Hell, Dani, the last time I was almost convinced I liked it."

Dani felt bile rising, racing up within her. She ate it.

"I am never ever going back, got it? So, I, we, just have to dot the i's and cross the t's on some plans see?"

Dani shook her head.

"My folks are untouchable, Dani. Sort of like your old man, right?"

This she understood.

"I know it, Thurber knows it. If he tried to nail them, they'd sue his ass off for false memory or something. Quit looking like that, Dani. I'm telling you that for all these years my mother thinks it was my fault. That has not changed." She slumped against the tree trunk. "That's never going to change, and I'm not putting myself in harm's way again. I am not going back, and the thing is, Kevin isn't either."

Kevin got up and circled the tree.

"See, as decent as his folks sort of are, they can't accept that . . . there's no way. . . ." She glanced at Kevin. "They're just going to keep readmitting him to places until he comes out a raving heterosexual."

Kevin poked his head around the trunk. "There's no chance, nada, that they can live with the idea that their Christian son is a Christian queer. They're praying on it as we speak."

The fist in Dani's stomach clenched.

"So to cut to the chase, we have to disappear. When I turned sixteen I came into a small stash that'll keep us until Kevin turns sixteen in a few weeks, and then he can collect welfare."

"You're running away?"

"There are schools, alternative schools in the city set up for kids like us. I worked it all out on the Net. We have to go under for a while because our very concerned families will have to put on an impressive-looking show of trying to find us but—"

"You're running away?" Dani was stricken and thrilled at the same time.

"We're going to be our own little family," said Kevin. "And, well, we know your mom's left your old man and everything, but just in case it doesn't, if it, if you can't trust . . . well you probably can't, so we were . . ."

"Hey," said Scratch, "my idea. My invite. Besides you're screwing it up. Dani, we may not be much, but we're safe. Kev and I have to go first because . . . well, because . . . ya know? But we could send you a code or let you know or . . . ae-a-r-r-g-h-h." She grabbed her hair in mock despair. "Danielle Webster, do you want to come with us?"

Come with them? Did she want to come with them? They were asking her! People were asking her about what she wanted to do. They wanted her. "Uh . . ."

"Thing is," Kevin reached for her, "you're under age. Someone would probably feel obligated to hunt you down, you know? So it would be better if you actually, well, got them to give you your walking papers."

She wanted to cry. If only she could remember how. "But you don't know anything about me. Nothing. And you want . . ."

"Hello!" Kevin snorted. "We've only been peeing in the same foxhole for two months. We know you, Dani."

Scratch stepped over to her. "See, you and moi are going to rebuild our trust in the male species. It's not much, I grant you, but we're going to start with Kevin and work our way up."

"Oh yeah! Reap this milestone." He jumped on her and they proceeded to roll around screaming at each other.

Dani hugged her knees.

"So?" Scratch spit out some grass.

"No one has ever . . ." She cupped her head in her hands, smiling at the aroma of clean grass. "If it weren't for Kelly, I'd . . ."

Scratch narrowed her eyes at Kevin.

"See, thing is, she doesn't have anyone but me, never has. You're right, I can't trust my mother, I mean, why would I? But I have to take care of Kelly for a little while longer. I blew it. I . . . I have to fix it if I can."

"That's cool." Scratch held up her hand. "Nothing's happening tomorrow. There's time, lots of time. We can talk about it later, okay?"

"Yeah." Relief washed over her. "Sure, later."

"Yeah," agreed Kevin. "We've still got time before . . . before what? Are we going to the Career Counseling thingy or the four o'clock movie?"

Dani jumped up. "I don't know about you guys, but I need a bath more than I need *The Sound of Music*."

Kevin and Scratch applauded wildly.

Scratch called out after her. "Feel free to use my—"

"I know, I know," Dani waved back, "your White Ginger bath goop. Thanks." She could hear them bickering as she made her way back to the Quad.

"I said it was too soon, but no . . ."

"Shut up, Kevin."

"You know, maybe her mom—"

"Shut up, Kevin."

"Whatever you say, *Scratch*."

"That's Alison to you," screamed Scratch. "It's definitely Alison. A-L-I-S-O-N!"

"Okay, so *please shut up, Alison*."

"Okay already. You just had to ask nice!"

By the time she reached the Quad, Dani was flying. They wanted her to come with them! They knew what she was and still and still . . . they wanted her.

If only it weren't for Kelly.

It always ended up being about Kelly.

Date: May 11
Time: 1:30 p.m.
Presiding Therapist: Dr. William Thurber
Patient: Danielle Webster
Transcript Code: 807-15

WT: Ready? And . . . okay, let's begin. First of all, Dani, I have to say that your last . . . umm . . . three, yes, three sessions have been very rewarding. I hope that you have a sense of that, too. I believe you're making a conscious effort to open up and it's paying off. I also think we've finally licked your meds adjustments, so that little vicious cycle has been toned down a bit. Frankly, I'm very, very encouraged.

DW: Wow. Well, yeah, I can really feel the results of this opening up and healing.

WT: Uh-hmm, I might also say that I'm still a tad puzzled by what could have brought this communication transformation about. However, one of my many gifts as a gifted therapist is that I'll work motivation any way I can get it.

DW: Yeah, well . . . I think maybe it's one of those "never look a gift horse in the mouth" kind of deals. Besides, I mean, what's to know? I want to get better, to heal and stuff, and eventually to leave here. Hey, if I didn't, I'd really be nuts.

WT: Okay, okay. I know you're a chess player. I've castled. I stand rebuked but nonetheless alert. Your mother is absolutely overjoyed. She said that your last visit was unbelievable. You talked about your . . . let's see, yes, about your friends, about Harold's new look, and about . . . uh . . . your French class here, right? She said it was miraculous.

DW: She said that?

WT: Yes, let's see . . . yes, very, very . . .

DW: Well, that's more of that healthy, healing stuff for you. I feel like I'm on a real roll. Friends, communication, opening up to my mother. Well, it just feels real real, you know?

WT: Yes, I think I do. Touché, Dani. Knight to Queen's Three.

DW: (blank) Huh?

WT: Dani, does this transformation have anything to do with your roommate? Has Section C's longest resident been co—

DW: Cooperating with me? Yeah. By the way, I think she's going to want to be called Alison again, but she can tell you herself, right? Has she been helping me open up? Yeah, sure. Well, you can imagine how it goes: Alison opens and Kevin heals. I'm like a one-man Tupperware canister. Ha-a! Just yesterday, in group, remember, I went on and on about my horrible piano recital thing? Whoa! I'm still drained, you know?

WT: Yes, it was impressive, especially the terminology!

DW: Yeah, see, so . . . what do you mean—the terminology?

WT: There are times when it sounds like you've swallowed the *Diagnostic and Statistical Manual of Mental Disorders.*

DW: (blank) Well, I need the words right to make you understand, is the thing.

WT: Maybe one day soon you'll come to believe that I want to—that I will—understand you in your own words, Dani.

DW: Did I do something wrong? Bad?

WT: Absolutely not. Dani, look at me. You're not capable of doing a bad thing. Until you're able to fully comprehend that, try to trust in my judgment of you. After all, I've built up an impressive speaking engagement list based on my judgment of issues like that.

DW: Well. Yeah, for sure. I couldn't agree more with whatever you just said. But until then, don't you really, really think, I mean, can't you just see how I'm slowly, well, not that slowly, I am mediumly, uh, re . . . reintegrating, that whole disparate memory–reality thing? Huh?

WT: (audible sigh) You've been spending too much time in the much disputed multiple personality disorder section of the manual.

DW: Oh, gotchya. So . . . what am I?

WT: Hurt, Dani. You're hurt.

DW: Well, yeah, I . . . there's that, too.

WT: Yes, there is. Hang on. I was reviewing your pediatric record this morning. They're . . . hmmmm . . . here they are, yes, spiral fracture left humerus, perforation of the right ear drum, a three-finger fracture, crush injury, and a *contre coup* fracture—that's a head injury, Dani.

(blank)

WT: We've never talked about any of these . . . injuries . . . about what led up to them. Would you like to . . . ?

DW: No.

WT: Perhaps if . . .

DW: That stuff healed. I'm as good as new.

WT: Dani, has Scratch—I mean Alison—been pumping you with her Seven Secrets to positing out Thurber?

(blank)

WT: Dani? You're bright enough to know that will only get you so far. Why are you so keen to get out all of a sudden? Is it because your mom has left your dad?

DW: But, *am* I getting better?

WT: Absolutely, you're making quantum leaps. Hear me on that. You haven't had a dissociative episode in . . . a very long time. But Dani, why are you trying to convince me that you're so desperate to join your mother in her new life?

(Audible sigh)

WT: Your friends? You never talk about your friends or a guy, a boyfriend maybe. Is there some guy out there, a best friend?

DW: Right. Zero there, too, but at least I know it, knew it. What I mean is that for the last little while, I don't know, year or so, I ran with the cool crowd. Okay, on the very edge. Let's face it, the only reason I was even within spitting distance was because I was nuts and I could out-drink anybody. That amused them. Mummy was thrilled. Don't go looking so surprised. As long as I was hanging with the "names," my mother cut me all kinds of slack. It happens all the time with parents. They haven't got a clue. They're just thrilled with Susie's social success. Meanwhile, Susie is hanging with users and losers. My best friends are in here. Pretty pathetic, huh?

WT: They're great kids, Dani. That you've linked into people like Kevin and Alison is in itself a testament to . . . Do you have to keep circling your chair? I'm getting a little dizzy tracking you. So the rush to go is . . . ?

DW: I have to take care of Kelly. Period. Full stop. And I'm sure you know why. I admit that it's mainly a guilt trip on my part, but you know, you have got to know, my mother will eventually cave . . . and well, what if Kelly is at Daddy's for a weekend or whatever he's made her agree to, and what if Daddy has one Glenlivet too many and . . .
(blank)

WT: Okay. Got it. But let me venture something I think you're ready for. I'm of the opinion that your mother . . . well, let's review. Almost two years of ALANON meetings, a year of weekly sessions with Dr. Amis, and she's been seeing Dr. Richardson steadily about your care. She left your father, Dani! Picked herself up and left. She placed you in here by herself and figured out how to neutralize him in the process. Can you . . . ?

DW: Yeah, yeah, yeah. I know all that and I know you're all impressed, but she's still got a pile on her mind, no matter how you cut it. Daddy's little punching bag is in here, right? What if she's running around with paint chips and . . . you haven't met him. He can be awesome, like, blinding really, and . . . Kelly . . . see, she sometimes wets the bed, you know? He . . .

WT: It's not your responsibility, Dani.

DW: A lot you know.

WT: When you come to understand that it's not your responsibility, never was, never will be, then you'll be ready for so much more.

(blank)

WT: Okay, let's try this on. You're so responsible, but you drank yourself into a state of alcohol poisoning not once, but twice. Your mother's guessing that you've been drinking for over a year. And that last time, Percodans. How is that being responsible?

DW: What is this—tough love all of a sudden?

WT: I use a variety of techniques. It keeps 'em guessing. How, Dani?

DW: She never knew.

WT: Who?

DW: I drank alone, in secret, in places away with my crew, or in the basement, or even in the ravine. Kelly never, ever knew. She's got to be hurting. I have to explain everything and make it up to her. You have to believe me. I was so careful. It was really, really important that she not know.

WT: I believe you, Dani.

(blank)

WT: Dani, you're blocking me again and we both know it. I know we're past that. So how about back to the opening and healing stuff? I can take a little manipulation if you can.

DW: Sure. Sounds like fun.

WT: Okay, then, you're extremely intelligent. All of your ERB and IQ scores have you running circles around Alison, and she's no slouch. Why do you hide it? Why is your scholastic performance so breathtaking in its mediocrity?

DW: There's lots of different ways to be smart.

WT: To get back at your father?

DW: No, I wasn't trying to punish Daddy. It wouldn't be enough.

WT: Then?

DW: It's also in the manual, Doctor. I found it the other day, standard issue stuff. Daddy is smart. Heck, Daddy is probably a genius. I, his injured so-to-speak progeny, want nothing of his. I reject it. I choose not be like him. Simple.

WT: It's not that easy.

DW: I didn't say it was easy. I said it was simple.

WT: Okay, now you've castled. Feel better?

(blank)

WT: Shall we try one more route before the end of the session?

DW: Open and heal. Heal and open. I aim to please.

WT: Can we talk a bit about the Game?

DW: Absolutely. General or specific?

WT: General.

DW: Metaphors, allegories, or symbolism?

(blank)

WT: Symbolism probably. I'm never too sure which of those is which.

DW: Ha-a! Fire away, but first I want it noted that Jared is crowding me. I don't think dear old Janice is enough for that boy. He needs more victims.

WT: What happened?

DW: This time? Kevin threw him against the wall. Actually. I think he liked it. Jared, I mean. Then Yolanda was there. Like, does she walk through walls or what? Anyway, she stared them both down.

WT: Are you afraid of Jared?

DW: No. No, that's a lie. But not so much for me lately, but I don't know, maybe Kevin. He . . . it's nothing I can point to exactly.

WT: And?

DW: And so tell the staff to watch Jared! I'm trying to get out of the responsibility–protection racket, remember?

WT: Touché again. You're scoring all the points, Dani. I'll alert Harold. Now, the Game . . . wouldn't you be more comfortable sitting down?

DW: Is it against the rules to stand?

WT: No.

DW: Then, I'll stand and while I'm standing and on a roll so to speak, well . . . I don't want to go to French class anymore either.

WT: Oh? What about . . . ?

DW: What about poor old Monsieur Aboud? Well, what about him? He's not my responsibility, you know, even if I'm the only one in his class. And . . . and he's probably not the best French teacher on the planet, and even if he were, I'd rather go to Spanish with Scratch and Kev. That is, if it's okay and everything. Okay?

WT: Whatever makes you comfortable, Dani. No more French.

DW: Really?

WT: Really. Would you like to talk about this a bit more or go on with the Game or . . . ?

DW: I'm cool with the Game stuff. Fire away.

WT: All right. So then, as I understand it, the constructs are quite elaborate. There are two warrior princesses, Sacred Groves, an aroma-based entry, a set pattern mystic world, Saraya, goodness personified, trapped. Could you at least stop circling? It's . . . making me want to light up.

DW: Okay, okay, no circling . . . occasional shuffling?

WT: Deal! So your Saraya was imprisoned by Yuras, who represents irredeemable evil. Your Game . . . the standard interpretation would be that Saraya is your mother as you remember her when you were very little, before she was imprisoned by your manipulative, controlling fath— You're rolling your eyes. You've picked up quite a few of Kevin's mannerisms.

DW: I like the way he dresses, don't you? Especially his shirts. I covet his shirts.

WT: Excuse me? No, don't explain. So Yuras stands in for the overpowering evil of your father while your mother, Saraya, is—

DW: Is at a never-ending Junior League meeting. Don't you pay attention?

WT: Try to entertain this for a moment. Your mother did break out of her prison. It worked, Dani. You broke her out. You saved Saraya. The Game, your Game—in the end it worked. Your mother is free!

DW: Well, good for her and fund-raising committees everywhere, but Mother was not Saraya. Now you're the one that's too reliant on the manual. We had rules. We, Kelly and me, didn't bring them into the Game in any way, shape, or form. We left them at the top of the ravine slope. It's right in front of you! You haven't been paying attention.

WT: But your mother—

DW: My mother nothing! For Godsake! Kelly was Saraya! Pure and good, sweet and weak. Come on, Kelly was always Saraya, get it?

WT: Kelly? But then . . .

DW: We left them behind, Dr. Thurber, at entry. It was only the two of us in the Game.

WT: I don't think I'm . . .

DW: Just us. Get it? We quested for us, for our souls. What better quest is there? It was my game. All mine. I am the strong one. Connect the dots. We both knew it. It was clear to us. Light and dark. We battled the dark. Kelly was the light. Kelly was good. I am bad. I deserved . . . I am the dark. He tried to beat it out of me. But I wanted to be good so much for . . . for everyone. Kelly knew. The quest, it was . . . to end the bad, the evil in me. And still it goes on and on and on. Don't you see? Kelly is Saraya. I am Yuras. Yuras must be vanquished. I want to be good, and you'll let me go when I learn how to be good, right? I want to be good.

(blank)

WT: Dani, look at me. You are good. You are very . . .

DW: I want to learn.

WT: I promise, we will all help you realize just how good you are.

DW: I want to be good.

(blank)

WT: Dani, your mother says that you are good through and through. All the time. Nonstop, she talks about how pure you are. Are you hearing this? She said you are good.

DW: She did?

WT: She did.

DW: That's good. Right?

END OF SESSION: 3:40 P.M.

May 14

They were in Kevin's room. He was without a roommate at the moment, and Dani was amazed at how much his room looked like Scratch's half of her room. No festering socks in the corner, no suspicious-looking underwear crawling out from under the box spring. She plopped herself on the bed nearest the window. "You two are going to make beautiful antiseptic music together. How can you even think of having me come to live with you guys?" Dani had sporadic moments of tidying, usually induced by much sighing and heaving from Scratch. But when all was said and done, her half of the room didn't look all that much better for the effort.

Kevin was carefully laying out five beautiful shirts on his bed. "Ah-h-h . . ." he said, returning the fifth to his dresser. "We plan to mold you tag-team style, while you're still fairly nuts and malleable." He turned to her, proudly pointing to his display. "Ta-da! Okay, pick. Must look lovely for mummy. I think these four would flatter your skin tone the most."

"Wow." Dani jumped off the bed and touched each shirt tenderly. "I mean, wow! Kevin, you could slice bread with your sleeve crease. How do you get them to do that for you? All my stuff comes back looking like a scrunchy."

He caressed the yellow silk she was holding. "They don't. I do. I iron."

"You iron?"

"Yeah, I brought my travel iron from home."

"Oh man, I didn't even know there was such a thing."

"Scratch comes in and irons, too. That's basically how we met. She covets my iron."

"Kevin," Dani said unbuttoning a pure white shirt with a raised leaf pattern, "Scratch only wears sweats. You don't iron sweats. Even my mother wouldn't iron sweats if she knew what they were."

"Scratch irons her sweats—how could you not notice?"

"I did. I thought it was the drugs."

Kevin held the white shirt against her. "Beautiful. I would've picked that one, too. Virginal, but knowing."

"Huh?"

"Never mind; your mother will appreciate it."

Dani couldn't stop stroking the sleeve. "It feels like a kiss."

"It's yours," he smiled. "Too small for me."

"Oh Kevin, thanks!" Before he could duck she kissed him. "Now, turn around."

"What for? I'm not going to maul you."

"Turn around! I could just be the one who transforms you."

"That's what they all say." He sighed and faced the window.

Dani whipped off her Riverwood T-shirt and donned the snowy white shirt. She looked at herself in the mirror and didn't flinch, didn't turn away. "Hey, Kev. Who'd you say I looked like, Katherine Hepburn?"

He turned around. "Audrey Hepburn, you dolt. Katherine Hepburn was number one on the AMC top one hundred actresses of all time. Audrey was in the twenties somewhere. Both dressed great, but Audrey had that whole gamine thing happening."

Dani turned and gave him a raised eyebrow.

"Yeah, yeah, yeah," he shrugged. "What else is a closeted Christian boy to do? I wasn't into war games and I hate computers. I had no choice but to perpetuate a stereotype," he said, sighing. "At least I never got into show tunes."

"Kevin, I have absolutely no idea what you're talking about."

He rewarded her with a noisy, forceful kiss to the forehead. "No, I know you don't."

Dani started practicing her repertoire of sincere smiles. They were coming along nicely.

Kevin rummaged around his night-table drawer and threw some emery boards at her. "Fix up your nails. It looks like you've been using them to open paint cans."

Dani looked at him hopefully.

"Uh-uh. I have my limits."

She dutifully sat down and began sawing away at her thumbnail while Kevin took the opportunity to rearrange his shoes and belts.

"Kevin?"

"Uh-hmm?"

"Aside from this really sick compulsive ironing thing, you're the most normal person I've ever met."

"Uh-hmm." He tossed her a braided leather belt. "There's no

buckle on that one. You just tie it, Fred Astaire–like, and it'll look great with your jeans. What's your point?"

"Well, why exactly are you here? I mean, I know your parents want to fix the gay thing, but I can't see Thurber buying that for a second. So is it because . . . well, I mean did you really . . . how exactly did you . . . uh . . . ?"

"Tried to hang myself."

"Oh God, Kevin!" The image that flashed before her was replaced by flashing lights, the ambulance lights. "What happened?"

"The cleaning lady found me in the garage and cut me down with a paring knife. Bless her fearless Filipino heart." He examined the belt he was holding. "I wasn't even stoned or anything. But it's like I keep saying in Little Group, I didn't see any other way out then. What I'm clear on now is that there is always, always another way out."

Lights flashed at Dani. Red, white, red. She shook her head. "You know what's amazing? No matter what . . . my father did, said, the booze . . . I never ever actually wanted to die, I mean I never wanted to stop . . ." She looked at him imploringly. "I didn't." She rolled up her sleeve cuffs. "I guess I have to live so I can get back at him."

Kevin sat on the bed opposite her. "Yeah?"

"Yeah." She folded into herself. "No. I think, I have to . . . I just want to hear him say that he's proud of me. Just once. Once would be enough." She admired her groomed thumbnail. "Yeah, once would be plenty."

"Dani . . ."

"I know, I know, self-entrapment, page 463 of the disorders

manual. Forget about it. What I don't get is your parents. Scratch says they really care, that they're sort of normal, God-fearing . . ."

"Like normal is in Scratch's vocabulary!" Kevin slumped in against the dresser. "It would almost be easier if they were rotten through and through like yours. No offense."

"None taken."

"I told them about a year ago that . . . that I was gay. I mean, times have changed, right?"

"And . . . ?"

"And they went, and still are, ballistic. What was life going to be like for me as an abomination in the eyes of the Lord, etc., etc.? Man, they trotted out to 'save' me before I even got the words out."

"And . . . ?"

"And three therapists, two evangelical miracle workers, one psychiatrist and I don't even know how many Zolofts, Lithium, and eye of newt stuff later, I had to stop it. And so . . . here I am with you and Scratch. And I am better. I know it and so does Thurber, *but* not well enough to go through more prayer meetings over my hell-fried faggot soul." He looked at her fussing with his shirt cuffs. "You look good, Dani."

Dani threw her arms around him, and he hugged back, hard. Absorbing her. His hug, it was the way Kelly hugged. She felt like a noodle dissolving into it.

"Dani, you okay?"

"Yeah, sure," she sighed. "It's just that I can't believe someone like you . . . well, that anyone would actually try to off themselves."

"Can't you?"

"No! Really I can't. I told you already—the booze and the pills that last time . . ." The flashing lights distracted her.

"That last time, Dani?" he asked gently. "You weren't anywhere before, you weren't partying, you were all by yourself in the house. You said so."

The blue walls of the basement pressed in on her. The incessant pattern of the ambulance lights, red, white, red. The memory of shame erupted along with the memory of the lights.

She couldn't do anything right. Idiot cow! Couldn't even . . .

"I don't know, Kevin," she whispered. "Maybe."

He draped his arms over her shoulders. "It's okay."

"When is it over, Kevin?"

"My theory or Thurber's?"

"You."

"Not ever." She turned away. "Not you, me, Scratch, Bobby, or Janice or even Jared. No matter what they say."

"But then what, Kevin? There has to be a 'better' than this, a 'better' than how I was before this. There has to be more than how I am now, please God."

He started to amble around the room. "The way I figure it is that whatever brought you in here, Dani, you got to face it. Square. And when you get out, you learn how to wear it."

"Huh?"

"Yeah," he nodded, "like some kind of invisible coat that you can't take off. It has to be on all the time, every single moment of your life."

This was so not what she wanted to hear.

"Okay, so sometimes it's too hot, and sometimes it's too heavy because, I don't know, it's wet with rain or something. But it's your coat. You learn to wear it. There'll be times when you don't even know you've got it on. And then sometimes there'll be a breeze and you walk around unbuttoned and it'll be okay. And then one day you'll be actually grateful, because it's just so unbearably cold and that stupid coat will save your butt." He smiled, delighted with himself. "Yeah."

Dani got into his pacing path.

"Do you get it?"

"I do." She stopped suddenly and they collided. "Sort of."

"I'm still working it all out in my head," he pouted. "I wasn't ready for a formal presentation."

"No. It's not that. It's . . . Kevin, I just don't know what my coat is."

Scratch burst in like a SCUD missile.

"Aw-w-h-h, did I break up a tender moment? Too bad. I'm here now; everyone pay attention to me. I am in distress!" She ripped open a large package of Skittles and began color coding them on Kevin's bed. "Okay, you guys can have all the green ones." Scratch had to have a new color to hate every day. Today, she couldn't bear green. Kevin and Dani divvied up their loot. "Hey!" Scratch beaned Kevin in the head with a raspberry Skittle. "I said I was in distress!"

He popped all of his candy into his mouth and mumbled. "And this is notable because . . . ?"

"I mean it. I just had my one-on-one. I have a feeling that insurance company is putting the screws to the clinic. I'm out of here soon, children."

Kevin lifted up his bedspread to reveal an overnight bag under the bed. "I'm ready anytime, precious."

Dani gasped, but Scratch was oblivious to her reaction. She circled Dani suspiciously. "Hey, what happened? You almost look good."

"It's the shirt," said Kevin.

The two of them were making her dizzy. She felt strong with them, but sometimes she couldn't quite get a foothold on the rhythm of their banter. Her head would swim with the effort of trying to fit something in.

"So, Danno, just how nuts are you still?" She was tapping on her wrist watch. "Can you speed it up? We haven't got forever."

Dani's heart raced. Flashing lights and—

"Alison, you can be such a pig!" said Kevin.

"Yeah, okay, sorry, sorry." Scratch rolled her eyes at Kevin. "Like who died and elected you Mr. Empath? No guff, Dani, you do what you got to do, okay? We won't dump you. Got it? Whenever you're ready, you're with us." She turned back to Kevin. "There is nobody more sensitive on the planet, once I put my mind to it." Making a face, she reached out to Dani and gave her a stiff little squeeze. "See! Like how caring is that?"

"Okay, you guys, I'm not some Victorian Rose or something. I get the score and I'll deal with it. But first things first. Right now, it's time to go and meet Mummy."

They strode three abreast down the corridors. Dani loved it when they walked like that. She imagined how confident and breezy they looked, like the opening shot of a cop show. She could just see the credits rolling underneath them: *The Avenging*

Angels, an Aaron Spelling production. The scourge of dysfunctional families everywhere.

A lady—her mother?—stood up to greet the Angels. She was wearing chinos and a sweater, her hair loose. No makeup. She looked like a kid.

"Hi, Mrs. Webster." Kevin reached out for her hand. "I'm Kevin; nice to see you again. We sort of almost met a few visits back. You've loosened up, I see. Looks good on ya. I think Lagerfeld has lost his grip on Chanel."

"Why yes." Her mother was flustered. "Thank-you. I think. I remember you. It was that first visit. You were hovering about." She smiled at him.

"And this is Dani's erstwhile roommate, Alison. She's only semicertifiable now. We all hold out great hope," he said gravely.

"Shut up, puffball," Scratch glowered at him. "Hello, Mrs. Webster. It's nice to meet you. Dani talks about you all the time."

"Oh?" Her mother's hands fluttered about uneasily. When was it, Dani wondered, that she had looked at her mother last? Really, really looked.

Mrs. Webster smiled shyly at Dani. "Hello, darling. You look like a million. You really do."

Dani didn't feel scared, not this time. Everyone waited for her to say something to her mother. She felt swollen with power. "Hi Mom, thanks. . . . It's Kevin's shirt."

"Oh, well, it's beautiful on you. Just perfect."

Pathetic really.

"It's too small for me." Kevin patted his stomach lovingly. "Haven't been paying attention to my fat grams. I've been a naughty, naughty boy. Well, we've got to toddle . . . there's basketweaving, beadwork, anger management . . . busy, busy, busy." He shook her hand again. There was a tense moment when Mrs. Webster went to shake Scratch's hand.

Scratch thrust out her hand in a goofy version of a stop signal. "Sorry. But that's part of the certifiable part. Not quite up to touching strangers in a strange land yet. Nothing personal. I'm making tremendous strides," she smiled. "We'll be groping like fools by the next time. Promise."

Dani couldn't stuff down the giggles.

"Yes, of course . . . I . . . uh . . ." Then she smiled again. "I'll have something to look forward to that next visit then."

An "Atta go, Mom!" escaped from Dani.

Kevin snuck Dani a thumbs up as he and Scratch turned to go. "Well, later. . . ."

Mrs. Webster tentatively put her arm through Dani's and whispered, "Did I pass, do you think?"

"I'll let you know."

Her mother turned to her. "So, young lady, can I buy you a cup of coffee, or something wonderful, bursting with fat grams? Could we do that, do you think?"

That was it. There was her power source. Dani realized that she could vaporize her mother right now. She could. It would be that easy. It would feel good. The rest of the commons faded around them. Her mother's hands fluttered, fussing with her purse, her pockets. Dani knew all the signs. Every movement betrayed her; the breathing too shallow, the neck tense, but her eyes . . . in her mother's eyes. Dani could . . .

"A coffee would be great," said Dani. "And maybe a doughnut, too. Heck, I need the fat grams. Wait till you see the cafeteria. The renovation is finally finished, and Scratch, I mean Alison, always says . . ." Dani glanced at her mother as they headed down the corridor. "Are you crying? You're crying and smiling. Will you stop? They give demerit points for Making A Parent Cry. Hey, it's not like we've just solved world hunger. Why are you crying, for Godsake?"

Mrs. Webster daintily retrieved a linen handkerchief and blotted her eyes. "Because," she sniffed, "it's going to be the best cup of coffee we've ever had."

Dani inhaled and adjusted her power, trying to shift it lightly. "Mother, we've never had a cup of coffee together."

"Exactly," said her mother.

Johnson, Lewis, Webster and Stanford
399 Park Avenue, Suite 1205
New York, New York 10043
Telephone: (212) 555-1200
Mark Leyland Webster Direct Line: (212) 555-1206

Riverwood Youth Clinic May 15
Riverwood, N.Y.
10621
Attention: Mr. Stephen Bedard
Chief Administrator

Dear Mr. Bedard:

This is further to our discussions of March 1st and April 15, 2000, wherein I confirmed that my medical health insurance company, Rockland Inc., would assume full responsibility for the payment of all hospital costs for my daughter, Danielle Webster, commencing immediately.

I have informed Dr. Thurber of this and have advised him that I will not be seeking custody of the child once she is released to outpatient status. Dr. Thurber has convinced me that pursuing custody at this time would not be in the best interests of the child. In view of the current extraordinary circumstances, my lawyers advise me that this decision will in no way limit my rights to pursue further custody issues and/or legal claims. As you are no doubt aware, I also met with Doctors Thurber and Richardson and as a result I have dropped my formal requests to see Danielle while she is under the clinic's care. Mrs. Webster has assured me that we will be able to reach some future amicable visitation accord. Your counsel should be apprised of the fact that Mrs. Webster has provided me with written confirmation that she will not be pursuing any baseless claims arising out of Danielle's initial therapy sessions.

The child has always displayed an unusually intense imagination. I am sure that Dr. Thurber will be able to attest to the overheated fantasies that we all had to endure involving a ravine near our house. That, coupled with our family tragedy, has made me reassess and appreciate that long-term care is what is called for in this situation.

My goal is to restore the child to good health. My hesitancy at the outset was due to a lack of familiarity with your clinic's fine reputation. Her mother committed her without my consent and, concurrently, initiated divorce proceedings. Since that time, I have completed due diligence on your facility and am entirely satisfied that it is the finest adolescent clinic of its kind in the Northeast.

Now that I have officially undertaken to fund Danielle's hospitalization expenses, let me take this opportunity to insist on the very best care possible.

Please understand that money and time are no object. I will privately reimburse you for any costs not covered by Rockland. My only concern is the health and well-being of the child.

Yours very truly,
Mark Leyland Webster

c.c. Mr. John Patrick Lewis
Mrs. Sandra Stewart Webster

May 23

"So what time is your session?" asked Kevin.

"Don't change the subject." Dani looked at him cross-eyed. "When, Kevin?"

They were at the oak tree. By now the tree had become like the table in the cafeteria, recognizably theirs. If one of them was needed for something and couldn't be found, Yolanda would belt out, "Have you checked that stupid tree?"

"A week," said Kevin, "two at the most."

"And neither of you trust me enough to tell me where?"

Kevin drew up his knees and hugged them. "I'm totally with Scratch on this. It would be way worse for you to know. When we're set up, we'll figure out how to get in touch. We've even got your mom's number, but I promise it'll be before you get out."

Dani frowned back at the clinic. "It's just that, sometimes, occasionally . . . okay, a lot . . . I get panicky. What happens if I start checking out again and end up in perpetual Game mode and you guys aren't here to bring me back?"

He stared at her across his knees. "We never once brought

you back, Dani. Not once. You did it by yourself, every time. You still don't get it, do you? We need you more than you need us. You have this thing about just seeing the good, the strong, and the smart. You make me want to live up to what you see." He stood up. "I don't think I ever had that."

"Really?" She looked up at him, squinting through the haze. "I do that?"

"You do that." He held out his hand. "Come on. Aren't you supposed to be in dysfunctional family fun now?"

"Yeah," she sighed. "Enough of this toying with my affections. Take me where I don't have to worry about affection. It's time to see my mother."

Family therapy sessions were always held in the Little Group conference room, which felt cozy in Little Group but cavernous with just the three of them. Dani could hear chuckling as she approached the doorway. Mrs. Webster was chiding Thurber about his chair. They looked embarrassed when she walked in.

"Hello, darling." Mrs. Webster stood, took a step toward her. "How are you?"

"Mother." They were just sitting around laughing, shooting the breeze like . . . like this wasn't what it was. "I'm fine, thank-you." Like it was some walk in the park, for Godsake.

Thurber reached over to the tape recorder. "Ready to rap, you two?"

Dani stiffened.

"Dani?"

"Would it be, like, some major setback if just for once we didn't have it down for posterity. No notetaking, no recording, no eyebrow raising. I'm sick of feeling like a picked-over biology experiment."

"Okay by me." Thurber flashed a smile. "But I'm not making any promises about the eyebrows." He was having trouble removing the cellophane backing on his Nicorette gum. Both women became transfixed by this ritual. Her mother gasped as he popped two separate pieces into his mouth. "So ladies, where should we start?"

"A two-Nicorette session?" asked Dani.

"Just a hunch," he said chewing. "I've also got a Nicoderm patch in case you guys get really weird."

Her mother looked appalled, which boosted Dani's spirits. "Okay, zen. Ver vere ve last, Herr Doktor?"

Chewing with gusto, Thurber turned to Mrs. Webster. "We were trying to understand your mother's actions, or lack thereof. Trying to build a bridge to empathy. To understand why she stayed. Why she chose the path she did. Is that fair?"

No one blinked.

"So," he said, defeated by the silence, "how are we all doing with that?"

"Well," snorted Dani, "to be perfectly honest I don't feel a bridge coming on."

"Dani, please," her mother reached over and touched her hand. Dani withdrew it as if she'd been pricked.

"Okeydoke," said Thurber. "No bridges so far. Can you express why, Dani?"

She shifted in her seat, thinking about Kevin and Scratch leaving. How long would they wait? "Do I get points for expressing?"

"Big points and you know it," he nodded.

"She lies like a rug."

Her mother shut her eyes.

"She's been trying to tell us she was afraid of Daddy, that he controlled her. She's been watching too many movies of the week. He never touched her. Did he? She was like this Royal Doulton figurine for him. He only saw her."

Her mother shook her head. "I was nothing, Dani."

"Yeah," nodded Dani, "nothing—only gorgeous and talented and rich and . . . loved. Loved! He worshipped you. You stayed because you chose him over us. You chose him over me! You *chose!*"

"No, no, baby, no." Her mother kept shaking her head. "You deserve answers and I want to give them to . . . I wasn't . . . couldn't begin to think in terms of choice. I stayed because . . . I still can't explain . . . over a year of therapy and I still can't really explain." She slumped in the chair. "I guess . . . see, I had no idea I deserved anything else."

"Oh, get off it."

Mrs. Webster got up and walked around Dani's chair.

"Sit down, Mother. It makes our shrink nervous to have his people wandering around aimlessly."

Thurber hunched over, clearly uncomfortable about not being able to record or take notes. "You haven't talked about this before, Mrs. Webster."

"No." She sat down again and demurely crossed her legs at the ankles, which looked a bit off since she was wearing baggy jeans and Nikes rather than her luncheon suit getup. "You see, my father, Grandpa, used to have a drinking problem. When I was little, it was worse." She shut her eyes again. "He was violent then. It was so loud. That was almost the worst part . . . he . . . they were so loud." She winced. "Crashing, broken things. He was never sorry. I don't even think he remembered half the time. My mother never gave him an inch though, no matter what the consequences. *She* fought back. God, it was loud. *She* never would've . . . but me." She looked disgusted. "By the time Mark . . . he owned me. He didn't even have to raise his voice, I was that spineless. He'd just get this look. The look was enough."

Dani knew that look, like an ice storm brewing in his eyes. The look was a warning. The look was always just before. Lights flashed in the room. Red, white, red.

Mrs. Webster sat back in her chair. "But the real truth is, I came to Mark as nothing. I was his creation from the beginning. He taught me everything. Not just how to walk and talk, what to wear, what to say, and how to say it, but what to read . . . think. People . . . people sought me out, wanted to be near me because of him." She shuddered. "And unlike Grandpa, darling, when Daddy was . . . harsh, he was so sorry, so tormented afterward. You're right. I think maybe he did love me." She shrugged. "Maybe still does."

She faced Dani. "I have so much to be ashamed of. I don't even know where to begin. You see, it wasn't only the fear that paralyzed me, stupefied me. I . . . I craved his approval. When

Mark approved . . . life . . . see . . ." She stopped and groped around for the words. "When he approved, he made life . . . no, he made me beautiful, intelligent, desired. It was such a powerful thing."

The room heaved in on Dani. Broken memories ripped through in fragments. Daddy being proud of her. She was only eleven when she won the All-County piano competition for fifteen and under. She had practiced and played above her head for over a year. It was an endurance contest more than it was talent. But it was worth it. That night she nailed it. She knew from her first note on. Daddy was on his feet as she caressed the last three notes. Her beautiful, gleaming father stood clapping—for her. She didn't see anyone else.

"Bravo! Bravo!"

It was like being bathed in sunlight. Everyone got up. It didn't matter. Daddy knew she had it and Daddy was standing.

"Bravo!"

Their eyes locked. His voice thundered above the applause.

"That's *my* baby."

His hand thumped his chest.

"*My* baby girl! Bravo, baby! Bravo!"

She would have sold her soul to relive that moment just once.

"Did he ever hit you, Mrs. Webster?"

"No, not me." Her mother seemed to fade before her. "A long time ago, before Dani even, he broke things. It was," she frowned, "it was very loud. The last time . . . he . . . the television was smashed into a thousand . . . I left." She whispered, "I actually left."

"And!" Now Dani got up and circled around Thurber. "Why

didn't you stay away, for Godsake!"

"Because he cried." Both Dani and Thurber leaned in, straining to hear her. "To see your father sobbing. He swore never to do it again. But that wasn't even it."

"Then what, Mother! *What?*" Dani glared at Thurber, who was rifling through his jacket pockets for more gum. "It's in your shirt pocket."

Mrs. Webster stared at them, not seeing. "He reminded me that I couldn't live without him, that I didn't exist without him. I'd been gone three weeks. He was right. I went back. *I was good.* He was never loud again."

Dani wanted to pick up a chair and heave it out the window or, better yet, heave her mother out the window. *"Loud?* No, he was never loud. How convenient that you didn't ever have to hear, Mother! So convenient for everyone."

Dani kicked her chair clear across the room and still the shards broke through. "When I was twelve, I missed that year's recital. Do you know why, Doctor?"

Thurber shook his head. He was still trying to free the Nicorette.

"Mother was shopping for my outfit. She was late. I was practicing. It wasn't good, I wasn't any good, I knew I couldn't pull it off again. But I tried, oh how I tried. Over and over, I kept screwing up. 'You are destroying that piece. Idiot! Stop playing.' I wouldn't stop. 'Stop!' I wouldn't. He slammed the lid down." Dani reached for her left hand and tenderly held it against her cheek. "My fingers . . ." She faced her mother. "We both swore it was an accident. I know you knew."

Her mother didn't lift her head. Didn't respond.

"You make me puke."

"Dani . . ."

"And getting hit was nothing, nothing compared to the waiting to get hit. *And* that was nothing compared to the fear that he'd start in on Kelly. Poor old Kelly. He never laid a hand on her, and she was more terrified than I was."

Thurber finally freed the gum, but it popped out and landed on the floor. Dani reached down and got it for him.

"Thank-you."

"You're welcome," she said.

Mrs. Webster watched the whole exchange like she was on the other side of a glass window. "Dani. You were . . . are . . . so tender." She stood up again. "You won't believe me. I wouldn't either. I loved you so much it was crazy. He knew and he despised you for it. It took me years to figure that out. Even after Kelly, it wasn't until you went to kindergarten really. Darling, surely, you remember something, anything of then. I read a million stories and then we made them up. We made forts in the back with leaves. We danced. You loved my singing. I sang and I sang. There was this one song you loved so—"

"Shut up!" Dani turned away from the images piercing in. *Lavender's blue, dilly, dilly. Lavender's green.* "I don't remember."

Tears spilled out of her mother, but her expression didn't change. She ignored the wet mess on her face. "He didn't actually start the 'disciplining' until you were five. It was this ferry trip."

"That I remember, thank-you very much."

"It was only you. Never Kelly." Mrs. Webster sighed. "You

needn't have worried about Kelly. God forgive me. I never felt the same way about her. Maybe I never let myself. So she was safe, you see. See? He aimed at me through you. Through every vile thing he said—the blows, the words—it was all meant for me. It's how he controlled me."

Liar formed and disintegrated in Dani's mouth.

She knew it was true.

The knowing was not bearable.

"Eventually, I became more perfect. More accomplished, more distant, and he approved." Now her mother was crying in earnest. Thurber retrieved a suspect-looking handkerchief and waved it at her. She ignored it, her face distorted, red, ugly. "I thought I was keeping you safe that way. But whenever . . . I don't know . . . whenever I wasn't accomplished enough or delightful enough or eager enough, he . . . oh God, Dani, I'm so, so . . ."

Not bearable.

Her mother convulsed with awkward sobs.

He taught them not to cry. Hated crying. Crying was for the weak. But Dani watched her mother as if she were on TV.

"I was trying so hard, can't you see just a little? Everything I had went into this . . . this pose. If I pretended not to care so about you, to put him back at the center . . . then maybe he'd leave you alone."

Then the channel changed to the afternoon before her last recital. They were all in the kitchen preparing an elaborate dinner for the celebration that was going to take place after her first recital in two years. She still felt a little sick. Her mother hovered between making yellow rosettes for her cake and feeling Dani's forehead. "Is your ear worse? You're feeling hot. It's time for your medicine." But in the excitement of all that icing and just being in the kitchen together and good, they forgot to get it. Kelly was twirling around to Mozart while Dani was standing on a chair itemizing dinner demands when Daddy walked in.

The sound was sucked from the room.

"Danielle, come with me now. Your mother and Kelly will meet us there." No one did or said anything. Sh-h-h-h . . . everything was still.

"Dani, please, please try to remember." Ugh-h-h, her mother was a wreck. "I couldn't, didn't know, couldn't figure out how . . . how . . . Dani, please, darling, please try, you have to, you must try to forgive me."

Dani was sweating like then, like that night. She was soaked through. She remembered worrying that she might damage his car seat with all that sweat. She knew it was coming. Was waiting. She saw the back of his fist from the corner of her eye. It took forever. The crack to the left side of her face, waiting, her ear crashing into the door handle. The blood and pus smeared all over the leather. Over her. He broke her right then. He broke her and she cried.

She examined her mother, all small and heaving mascaraed tears. "I must? I must? Aren't you ashamed even to ask?" She stood up. "Forgive you? Forgive you! You were my mother. You were supposed to protect me! I *must* nothing. How could you, how *dare* you ask."

"Dani, oh darling, Dani please . . ."

"Shut up! Shut up!" Dani got up. "Crying is for losers, Mother."

Dani checked her watch. "Four-thirty-six, end of session. I'm willing to note this as a bit of a setback." She strode out of the room, slamming the door so hard it opened again. She could hear her mother sobbing all the way down the hall.

It felt good.

May 29

Dani waited for days for some expression of disappointment about her behavior in family therapy. She practiced remorse. Dr. Thurber appeared to be particularly preoccupied that whole week. Bored by her constant fretting and desire to dissect the whole session again and again, Kevin and Scratch kept telling her to get over it. It was a nonevent to everyone but her. But she couldn't stop worrying about how much that outburst had set her back. It was a stupid mistake. She had let the bad part get out. They saw it. Thurber was probably disgusted. By the time Dani bumped into Thurber on the way to Friday's Career Day Lecture, she'd convinced herself that she was going to be institutionalized for life.

Dani heard him before she saw him. The wheels on his trusty chair had been getting progressively worse. It sounded like he was torturing piglets every time he went somewhere.

She waited for him by the water cooler feeling like a stalker.

"Oh hey, Dr. Thurber. What's up? I'm just on my way to Career Day. I think I'm finally starting to really get something out of those lectures, you know?"

"Hi, Dani," he called. "Staff meeting." He made a sharp turn toward the boardroom and expertly snatched up two crammed file folders before they hit the ground.

It was hard not to laugh. "You're pretty quick for such a big shrink."

"Well, you've found me out," he sighed. "You see the bumbling but gentle psychiatrist is but a guise to comfort you troubled teens. But sometimes I let my guard down and my lightning reflexes and rapier wit escape quite by accident."

"Your secret's safe with me. Speaking of secrets . . ."

"Yes?"

"Uh . . . well," she winced. "Nothing really about secrets so much, but at family therapy . . . well . . . I was . . ."

"Great."

"Yeah, see, I am just so sorry. I don't know where that all came from, maybe the meds. . . . Did you say great?"

He grinned broadly. "Congratulations, Danielle Webster. Now that was an honest breakthrough."

"It was?" She slumped against the water cooler. "All this time I thought . . . I thought. Okay, so," she rubbed her forehead, "it's a deal with your anger thing, or . . . an expression thing. I just didn't, I mean, like I hurt her, which felt real good at the time but then . . ."

Thurber was making faces at her. She now recognized this as his way of not interrupting while encouraging her to finish a thought. "I thought you were going to throw away the key."

"You've got the key, Dani." He placed a beefy paw on her shoulder. His hand felt warm and light. "And you're ready to use it."

"Shrink metaphors!" she groaned. "We've made it all these

months without shrink metaphors, and now he plies me with shrink metaphors!"

"Come now, this from the clinic's finest linguist?"

"Hey!" She struck a pose. "I can walk the walk and talk the talk, but it don't mean I understand a thing."

"In that case," he pushed his chair into the room, "you'll make a first-rate psychiatrist. Oh, by the way, warn everyone that the lecturer, some Wall Street guru, had to cancel, so Miss Wissner is going to fill in."

"Aw, come on, not Miss . . ." He shut the door and deserted her.

Miss Wissner was the clinic's life skills instructor. Problem was, she didn't have any. Worse yet, she was completely incapable of even baby-sitting a class if Jared was in it.

Jared was feeling particularly expansive. Although he couldn't string two words together without one of them being a curse, he made up for it with particularly graphic body language. No other instructor would have stood for it. Miss Wissner just gripped her clipboard tighter and smiled nervously at him. Janice just looked at her shoes. Dani nudged Kevin's gaze toward her. "What's up with Janice? She looks like a whipped puppy."

"He's tired of her," Kevin whispered. "That's not good, not good for anybody."

Jared kept cranking up the volume, smothering everyone with his stream of consciousness about blow-job cops, corrupt parole officers, and his never-ending needs never, ever being met. No one interrupted.

After twenty minutes of nonstop gagging gestures, Scratch could no longer be contained. She helpfully offered that Jared was a spoiled deviant turd who didn't deserve to draw breath, let alone get a need met. It all happened in a heartbeat. Jared didn't even look at her. Instead, he went straight at Kevin and, without pausing, kicked his chair out from under him.

"Aw look, the faggot fell."

Was he drooling?

"Bend over, honey," he slurred. "I'll help you up."

They were all on their feet. Scratch was tripped by Janice. Dani leaped up and jumped on Jared's back. He shrugged her off like a sweater. Chairs were overturned. Jared lunged for Kevin. Somewhere in this commotion, Miss Wissner had the presence of mind to call in the cavalry.

The door hit the wall like an earthquake.

Harold was shockingly graceful for someone so muscle-bound. To watch him pick up Jared by the shirt collar was a thing of beauty deeply appreciated by everyone except, maybe, Jared.

"Do ya want ta have me impart my life skills all over your face?"

Jared, who was quickly turning into an eggplant, squeaked out a "No."

Harold grasped just a tad more of Jared's shirt collar and delicately cupped his left hand over his multipierced ear. "Pardon?"

"No sir, eaurghhh. No, thank-you, sir."

"That's betta," smiled Harold. "How about you, me, and the lady prof here go round up the doc?"

"But I—"

Harold torqued up his grip on Jared's neck. "Pardon?"

"Yes sir," croaked Jared.

Still clutching Jared, Harold waved everyone else off. "Dis class is dismissed. You kids go and frolic until your next . . . whatever."

"Aren't group dynamics an amazing thing?" said Kevin.

"Kevin. Oh my God!" Dani went to him, but Scratch was warding her off with the evil eye. "Kevin, are you okay?" It was as if all the blood had drained out of him.

Scratch was mouthing *not now* to her.

Kevin checked his shirt. "Get a grip, Dani. I've been through worse."

"Sure you have." Scratch cuffed him in the head. "You would have had his balls for breakfast if Harold hadn't interrupted."

Kevin nodded. For once he wasn't blushing. You could barely see his freckles. Scratch glared at Dani.

"Yeah." Dani finally agreed. "You would've nailed him but good all right. Bad timing on Harold's part."

Bobby was still hovering about looking like he was going to burst into tears. "Get lost, Bobo. We're going to the commons now."

"Scratch!" Kevin and Dani groaned in unison.

"Okay, okay! You can join us for dinner, Bobo," she called after him.

"Thanks, Alison," he yelled from the hall.

"At least he remembers." She surveyed all the upturned chairs, orphaned pads and pens. "Let's blow this place, children."

The commons lounge was deserted. "They must all be quaking in their rooms," shrugged Scratch. The three of them settled into the AMC afternoon movie. "What the heck is this?" demanded Kevin.

"Where The Boys Are," said Dani. "Me and Kelly . . . we used to love the way Connie Francis—that's the dark little busty one—sings the title song."

"Well, it sucks and she sucks, too." He shifted uneasily in his chair.

"What's up, Kev?" Scratch asked without taking her eyes off of the TV.

"Nothing. It just sucks, okay?"

Scratch moved over, closer to him and whispered. "Give it up, boy. What hits you hits me and Dani. Are we together or not?"

Me *and* Dani. Dani would've felt great if she didn't feel so bad. "There's more, isn't there?" Dani asked. "More with Jared. Kevin?"

A couple of anorexics walked in shivering despite their forty layers of clothing. Scratch stared them down until they went and hid in the far end of the lounge.

"Well, Kev? Is Dani onto something?"

"Uh-huh." He grunted. "Past couple of weeks, I felt like I was being stalked. It's him. I don't know what it is exactly, but it's bad. One night . . ."

"Yeah, one night . . ." urged Scratch.

"One night, it was late. I was asleep and I just knew to wake up because something was wrong. It was dark and I didn't turn around, but he was in there, in my room. I could feel him, I . . . could smell him."

"Oh. My. God! Jared?" Dani recoiled into the seat. "What did—"

"Nothing. I didn't move. I could feel him in there though. I heard him breathing. I just prayed my guts out, and after forever he changed his mind or got spooked or something, and left. I think he knew I was awake."

"Oh man," Scratch shuddered. "Damn, double damn."

"If anything happens . . ." Kevin turned to Dani. "I'm the queer, I'm the pervert. Victim or victimizer . . . it won't make any difference, and there's nothing Harold can do about that."

Scratch leaned over. "So now what, Musketeers?"

"You've got to get out of here," whispered Dani. "Sooner."

Kevin and Scratch nodded at each other. "Done."

The three of them locked back onto the TV screen as if it were a lifeboat.

"See the blonde one?" Dani's voice was wobbly. "We missed the part where she was struggling over whether to lose her virginity to George Hamilton—the tanned guy."

"She looks like a nun!" Kevin griped. "And him . . . yuck!"

Scratch rolled her eyes. "You are such a snob."

Dani ploughed right on. She had found that this was her most effective technique for dealing with not understanding what was going on with them. "Well, amazingly enough, that actress made, like, one more movie, and then she left Hollywood to join a religious order. She is a nun to this day."

It worked again.

"No way!" Scratch was in awe. She searched the actress's face for incipient signs of holiness.

"I don't believe this!" groaned Kevin.

"Oh, air out your pecker," said Scratch. "It's a great little movie. Not everything has to have subtitles, you know. Behave."

They watched the rest of the movie in companionable silence.

"You know, I don't think I ever watched a single movie with anyone from my family," Scratch complained. "Not one stinking movie."

"Yeah, yeah, yeah," said Kevin. "There's not an aspect of your pathetically melodramatic childhood we haven't mined to death."

Scratch looked like she was going to execute him.

Dani was trying to pay attention to the movie host describing the next feature. "Great," she said. "It's *Parish* with Troy Donahue and Connie Stevens."

"Didn't we just sit through her?" moaned Kevin.

"That was Connie Francis."

"Hey, I'm on to something," Scratch hissed. "A real family sits down and watches movies together even when it's not their favorite movie. Just sitting there, you know? You don't have to have a big hairy discussion, just being there in the same stupid room—that's what a family's about."

"About just being together, you mean," said Dani. "Right?"

Kevin ignored both of them. "Who is the blonde with the eye-liner? She looks familiar."

"Connie Stevens—the Home Shopping Network," said Dani.

"Right!" Scratch thumped the sofa arm. "Wow, she was an actress before she started selling all that stuff?"

"I need a suppository," complained Kevin. "You two are making me constipated. Ae-a-r-r-g-h-h! Alison, I know what this is about. We will be a family, got it? Whatever it takes. We'll do it, okay?"

"Won't it be grand?" smiled Scratch.

Dani curled into the corner of the sofa. It finally dawned on her. They were like her after all. No different really. Even together they were afraid. Kevin and Scratch were actually afraid. Afraid of going. Afraid of staying. Afraid of being left behind. Afraid, just like her.

June 1

Dani peeled into her room. She had just liberated another shirt from Kevin's collection and was eager to try it on before Little Group at three o'clock. The curtains were completely drawn. It was like walking into a blanket. She hit the lights and screamed at the same time.

"Aaeeeogh!"

Scratch was kneeling by her bed, hands clasped, head down. It looked like she had keeled over. Dani scanned for signs of blood. "Scratch. *Scratch!*"

Scratch looked up squinting at the light. "Alison," she said wearily, "it's Alison, dammit. I'm going to tattoo it on my forehead."

"Yeah. Sure. Whatever." Dani was hyperventilating. "You okay? I mean, what are you doing? It's dark and everything. Why is it dark?" Dani was inhaling her words. "What are you doing?"

"Praying."

"What?"

"You heard me."

"Yeah, but . . . come on. I mean really. You scared the . . . poop right out of me."

"Poop?" Scratch shook her head. "We've been together over three months and the best you can muster up is 'poop'?"

"Yeah, well," Dani shrugged. "How long have you been praying?"

Scratch snorted. "You should see your face." She got up. "People who have stumbled in on me while I was turning myself into a Cuisinart have looked less freaked out. The situation fairly drips with irony, don't ya think?"

"It's not that." Dani plopped onto her bed. "It's . . . the room was dark. I thought it was empty. I mean, come on . . . like, since when do you pray, especially secret praying. Is it a secret? Why didn't you tell me? I mean . . . you pray?"

"Dani, I've been to a thousand different Catholic boarding schools. It's like the old saying. You throw enough spaghetti on the wall, some of it's bound to stick."

"Wow," said Dani. "I didn't know that about spaghetti or about the Catholic schools. Sorry, I should have known. About you, I mean, not the spaghetti."

Scratch ignored her. "I saw Steve this morning."

"I know," said Dani. "Is that why you're praying?"

"No, you dufus. I was praying because I pray."

In all her months at Riverwood, Dani had never met or seen any of Scratch's family. No visits, no family therapy, just the occasional phone call. Even Kevin had only seen her mother once. But Dr. Steve kept popping up. He wasn't married, so he kept kind of a flaky schedule. He wouldn't come around for weeks, then come four days in a row. Scratch said that he stayed single all this while because he saw close up what marriage had done to his best friend, Alison's dad. Anyway, there he'd be, looking awkward and out of place, but at least he was there. Kevin was all for introducing him to Dani's mother.

"Okay, so how was Dr. Steve?"

"He's a dermatologist," Scratch answered.

"Uh, yeah, I know that, Alison." Without even realizing it Dani swept the room for signs of knives or pills or something. "Are you sure you're okay?"

Scratch started to pull up the sleeve of her left arm. It wasn't easy because she had to yank up her sweatsuit sleeve and then push up the turtleneck sleeve on top of that. The effort seemed to tire her out. She sat down on the edge of her bed.

Dani unclenched her stomach to make room for the nausea, but she didn't gasp or cry out. She thought nothing could be more shocking than seeing Scratch praying.

She was wrong.

Wordlessly, they both examined the angry, bubbling, raised welts, the long ragged lines, the symmetrical circles. Her arm looked like she had been chewed up by a cultivator. Dani instinctively sought out the markings from all the instruments Scratch had described in Little Group. There and there, the half moon markings of cuticle scissors; over here and here and here, erupting wounds from serrated bread knives. The neat markings were panic attacks when she didn't have anything better than a fork. And the circles, all those circles—cigarette burns.

Every inch of her arm was ravaged.

"This part is a bit worse than the others."

Dani finally exhaled and nodded.

"Steve says—and well, actually, Dr. Thurber gave me the idea—but Steve agrees, that plastic surgery will really fix this up. Too gross for words, huh?"

Dani felt like she was losing her battle with the nausea. She knelt beside her friend. "Can I? Alison, would you mind if I . . ." Scratch didn't move.

As tenderly as she could, Dani caressed her forearm. Rage ripped through her as she traced the crazy quilt pattern of welts and scars. Her hand trembled. "Oh God, Alison. How could you stand the pain?"

Scratch looked down at Dani as if really seeing her this time. "Stand it? I couldn't not stand it." She ran her forefinger across the longest welt. "This little pain stopped the big pain, the unbearable bits. At least for that moment. See?"

Dani thought about lying or joking, anything not to feel so stupid and useless. "No, I can't." She shook her head. "I wish I could. I really, really want to understand, but I don't."

Scratch sighed and stared at her little night table. "I was at this real swish clinic in Arizona. That was . . . uh . . . two places ago. They even had a little wing for mutilators, a real high-tech, this-minute kind of place, you know?"

Dani nodded encouragingly, even though Scratch wouldn't look at her. "Like D Ward here for the anorexics?"

"Yeah, but they had all the bells and whistles—only they didn't have Thurber and his crew. I got to tell you Dani—it's like Yo always says—the man's a mensch."

Dani nodded again.

"Anyway, there were lots of cutters, if you can believe it, and this one girl. She didn't cut—she yanked. It's another name, Tricky-something. She plucked out all her hair. No eyelashes, eyebrows, arm hair, nothing."

"Oh man."

"Yeah," Scratch smiled to herself. "And I remember thinking what a suck she was. Like what kind of relief could you get from that kind of crap? I thought it was more like a bad habit." She shook her head. "I was such a jerk to her. I had to cut to survive the next minute. I couldn't not or I would explode." She faced Dani again. "It's like when you'd leave for the Game. You said you couldn't not leave. You couldn't stop it. I understood, Dani. I understood even before you could explain it properly." She glanced back to her arm. "But that was then, as they say. Only . . . only . . . look, Dani. Look what's left." Tears welled in her eyes. "I make myself sick."

"No, Alison, don't. They're battle scars." Dani gently stroked her arm. "It's like this war took place all over your body. But you won, Alison. The only thing I really understand is that you won and then you helped me win."

Scratch shut her eyes. "Oh, Dani, if only, oh . . . crap!"

Dani was thrown by her anger. Perplexed, she began again. "Hey. Dr. Steve is absolutely right. I know plastic surgery will fix it and the other scars, too. And . . . and . . . what's left will fade away. I mean, most of my mother's friends look twenty-four, for Godsake! My mother will get you the names of the best guys on the planet. You name it: New York, L.A., Rio, wherever and whatever."

"Yeah?"

"Sure! Liposuction, lip injections, laser peels, dermabrasion, botox in the forehead, and stuff you've never even heard of."

"Hot diggety. While I'm at it I'm going to buy myself some breasts!"

"You want 'em," Dani grinned, "you get 'em."

"Na-a-a-h," she smiled. "I get into enough trouble without them. What's that scrunched up in your hand?"

"Oooh, darn." Dani jumped up. "It's one of Kevin's shirts. It's this celadon green. I think it suits my complexion a whole lot better than his. What do you think?" She whipped off her T-shirt and tossed it into the corner that was already breeding weeks worth of clothes.

"What do I think? I think you're a pig. Look at that." She waved at the pile. "You got clean laundry, dirty laundry, and half of Kevin's wardrobe in there." She glanced at Dani admiring herself in the mirror. "I guess that color looks okay on you."

"Great. I want to look fabulous as I dazzle my fellow inmates with my progress today."

"You'd look a tad more 'dazzling' if you ironed that shirt." She rolled down her sleeve. "It looks like you slept in it."

Dani beamed. They were back to themselves. "Oh lighten up, will ya!"

"Right!" snorted Scratch. "This from someone who says *poop* when she wants to cuss? We better go."

They both started for the door, but then Scratch turned back. "Hang on a sec." She ran over to her night table and snatched something out of the drawer. Dani bit down a gasp. The drawer was completely empty. "Can't leave without my luckiest charm." She held up the Old Man and the Sea key chain that Dani had given her a lifetime ago.

"Hey," Dani smiled at him, "you kept him?" She watched Scratch tuck him into her pocket. She had forgotten all about him. About giving him to Scratch. It was just a bribe then, the story and the key chain, a bribe to buy peace, buy friendship. Just like her father had done to her. She tried to dodge that truth but couldn't. She was ashamed about how well it worked both times, in the getting and the giving. "Do you always carry him?"

Scratch hit the lights. "No," her voice cracked in the darkness. "Just when I think we really need him. Let's go, Dani girl."

June 1, 3:00 p.m.

Dani and Scratch planted themselves on either side of Kevin in the Little Group circle. Dani felt a power surge. It was the first time she wasn't the one in between. She had been transformed—no, re-evolved—from protectee back to protector. *Yes!* She scanned the bank of windows and smiled at her Please Help the Blind blind. Then Jared oozed in. Rather than take his customary saved spot beside Janice, he sat directly opposite Kevin. Janice immediately began to pout and whimper. She slithered over to Bobby and begged him to change spots so she could sit next to her sun king. Despite the commotion, Dani still caught Jared's almost invisible little kiss thrown to Kevin.

"Where the hell were you last night?" Scratch hissed at Kevin. "I checked in every hour."

Kevin molded himself into the molded plastic. Dani felt the power surge ebb. Would they have taken off last night? Last night?

"I was with Bobby in the commons most of the time," he whispered. "Then Harold and me got into an all night

Dungeons and Dragons again. Did you see him?"

"You bet your ass, if you catch my drift." Scratch hunched over. "He was looking for a courting all right. Did you tell Harold?"

"Are you nuts?"

"Please sir," Scratch harrumphed. "You forget yourself."

Thurber cleared his throat. "Okay, ladies and germs, any immediate gripes or crises we want to share before we really get into it?"

"Yeah, sort of." Bobby hugged himself. "Kevin helped me with this last night, and I would like to-to-to just say it." Everyone turned to Bobby, which seemed to unnerve him. "What I just want to say, here, is that-that-that . . . don't take this bad or anything, but family therapy is sort of completely useless."

Everyone clucked sympathetically. Family therapy was right up there with root canal for just about everyone in the room. "See, basically, I'd rather go back into Isolation than watch my-my old man pacing and doing a slow burn for another ninety minutes."

Scattered "You bets" and "I'm with you there" percolated around him.

Bobby looked fortified by the sympathy. "I guess, I know I-I have to go and everything. I just wanted to say that it sucks. I needed to say that, and I said it, and I feel better for saying it is-is all."

There was considerate nodding just about all around.

"Well, I agree totally with Bobby," Dani heard herself say. "But thing is, maybe you shouldn't give up on it. I mean the point is that it could one day, eventually, maybe even mean something."

"Well, another Third World country heard from," drawled Jared.

"Piss off, lizard legs." This was Scratch's standard reply to anything Jared had to say these days.

"What I mean is, it could get better as Bobby gets better and learns to cope with his dad's . . ."

Everyone was looking intently at Dani.

"What is this crap? The Ice Princess spews up some drivel for the first time in weeks and you all look at her like she's the Dalai Lama."

"Yeah," Janice grunted. "You get to say stuff only when you finish up with the Sara chick and that whole bondage thing you were into."

Thurber seemed to note the group's agreement as he rifled through sheaves of papers. "It's a fair point, Dani. You've been granted the floor. It seems you've got a lot of catching up to do." He found the notes he was looking for. "Are you up to closing that piece, that . . . uh . . . last Game, for us before we take in your thoughts on the merits of family therapy?"

"Good idea," said Scratch. "I, for one, want to know how it all ends."

This was going way wrong. Dani was primed to show off her mature and healthy grasp of how the universe worked. Instead, she just felt like she'd been sucker punched. "Well, it's not relevant really. My point is to Bobby." She smiled at the poor guy, who by now was so mortified that he had put her in this spot, he would've run off skipping hand-in-hand with his father. "The thing is that it gets better if you let it, you know?" No one was nodding. "Like I'm so much better, like sometimes, people do . . . uh . . . change."

"Yeah, yeah, yeah," said Scratch. "So finish that Game thing and prove it."

Dani glared at her. "I haven't had an episode for weeks."

"And so you can't remember?" offered Kevin.

Thurber popped a Nicorette into his mouth. "It's okay, Dani. If you're not ready we can . . ."

"No! I mean yes. *Fine.*" What the heck was going on? Why was Scratch turning on her? Her roommate looked like a corpse. Did she pull an all-nighter? Was it the praying thing? Something was up. The hairs on the back of Dani's arms stood on end. "Okay, so where was I?"

Thurber rifled through more notes. He raised his hand. "Looking. I'm . . . ah-h! You and your sister were walking back toward home . . . because she had to get ready for a . . . yes, here . . . for a piano recital."

Dani nodded. "Yeah."

"Stand up," said Scratch.

"Up, up, up," chanted a couple of the kids.

Scratch avoided eye contact.

"Right, well, there's not much else. We were walking home. We talked about plans for the next time, that I'd do the Lavender song and the whole Binding Ceremony thing. We got past the tall grasses, and then we started up the hill." She could hear her heart beating. "Kelly kept screwing up and goofing around, you know? I got annoyed. I didn't want her looking all scratched up for her recital."

"You yelled at her?" asked Thurber.

"Well, not so much yelled. I just didn't want her to get in trouble. To get us in trouble."

"Admonished her?"

"Admonished is better," agreed Dani.

"Like any parent would or should?"

Dani started to sweat in rhythm with her heart beating. "I wouldn't know about that. Anyway, we finally got up. Got back on our bikes. Raced home. Got changed and went to the recital. End of story." She grinned at the circle of bored faces, terrifically pleased with herself.

"End of story?" said Scratch.

"Yup." She shrugged. "Pretty much, yeah. See, thing is—in the end—it was just a game, you know? Two scared little girls making up a . . . I don't know, a world where we could be the powerful ones."

"Hey," complained Janice, "how come she sounds like the doc all of a sudden?"

"Give it up, Dani," said Scratch.

Dr. Thurber cleared his throat. Protocol had now been breached. A lot of Little Group's rules were unwritten and unknowable. Yet if a line was crossed somehow everyone recognized the signs. Smelling blood, they perked right up.

"How was the recital?" asked Scratch.

"Fine," said Dani through clenched teeth.

"Fine? It was fine? Are you sure, Dani?"

What was happening? Dani had had a plan. She came in with ideas to show, to prove . . . She heard herself breathing, too loud. Not good. Each breath filled up the room, crowding everything else out. Could anyone else hear her breathing? Could they see . . . red, white, red . . . flashing safe, not safe, safe.

"Who went with who, Dani?" asked Scratch.

"I can't remember." Static. The air crackled. "It doesn't matter."

"Was she good?" asked Thurber. "Your sister, at her recital . . . was Kelly good?"

"Sure."

"Better than you?" asked Scratch.

Better than her? Kelly better than?

"No."

"No?"

"No." The ambulance lights flickered red, white . . . Dani shut her eyes to make them disappear. "I mean, yes, maybe. I don't know."

"Why, Dani," Thurber asked gently, "why don't you know?"

"I don't think . . . I, uh . . ." She sat down and surveyed the circle. She had everyone's complete attention. No one was pretending. Red, white, red, white, red. "When we came home from the Game, Mom was in the kitchen preparing a little party for after."

"Dani, think!" It was Scratch.

"We baked that day." Dani enunciated every syllable. "And we were all in the kitchen." She stood back up and faced her friend. "It was great."

Scratch's eyes welled up. "That was *your* recital, Dani."

"No," Dani shook her head. "Maybe I wasn't feeling well. My ear . . ." She cupped her ear tenderly.

"That was *your* recital, Dani." Scratch rubbed her face with both hands. "What happened at Kelly's? That last time. Kelly's recital, Dani."

"I . . . had a fever. . . ." The room filled with Dani's panic and held it.

Scratch reached into her pocket and retrieved the Old Man and the Sea key chain. She stood up and held it out to Dani.

The air grew thicker. It was too small a room for all that air and all that fear. "Alison, why?"

"You know why, Dani. You wanted me to." She clutched the key chain. "You wanted me to, or you wouldn't have given him to me."

"No." A little girl pleaded. Dani shook her head. "No. Please, Alison, Scratch, please don't."

"It rattles. It's always rattled, Dani. It drove me crazy. I thought something was broken in it somewhere." They both stared at the key chain. While everyone else craned their necks, bewildered as to what the heck was going on. "But you knew that, didn't you? I searched and searched and finally, ta-da!" A little drawer popped open from the bottom of the egglike container. "A secret compartment."

"Don't. Don't." Dani slid to her knees as a tiny bit of paper fluttered out to the floor. Scratch retrieved it and unfolded what looked like a newspaper clipping.

"Alison, I'm begging you."

Scratch implored her friend to go on. No words were exchanged but everyone heard the conversation.

"Alison . . ."

Scratch froze. Everyone froze. Finally, she slumped down

beside Dani. Everyone leaned in. "Okay, Dani, okay. Don't . . . don't be scared." Again her eyes welled up and angry tears spilled out. "Oh God, don't be afraid of me. I couldn't stand it."

Dani counted off the seconds by the thumping of her heart. Sixty-four, sixty-five . . . tired . . . if only she could lie down. With a trembling hand, Dani reached over to Scratch and slipped the clipping out of her fingers. She couldn't control the shaking. Dani rose, using the chair for support. "I don't . . ." She cleared her throat.

> AP-TRAGEDY STRIKES PROMINENT NEWBERRY FAMILY
>
> Westchester County N.Y., June 11—The Jaws of Life could not save 11-year-old Kelly Webster after a speeding Suburban overran a stop sign and hit Mr. Mark Webster's late model Mercedes. The accident took place at 10:30 P.M. on the intersection of Valley Rd. and Pondfield Ave. Mr. Webster and his daughter were returning from the Rockland County Music Festival in which Miss Webster had placed fourth.

Someone gasped. Dani looked over glassy-eyed. "It surprises you, too, eh? Only fourth." She soldiered on in a voice that no one had heard before.

> Seventeen-year-old Bruce Murphy was arrested and charged with vehicular manslaughter and will be remanded to the county jail as soon as he is released from hospital. "I don't even think that side air bags would have

> helped," said Donald Tremont, chief of rescue operations. "There just wasn't much of the poor kid left. It's a miracle that the father is alive." Mr. Webster, a prominent Manhattan attorney, former Councilman and current chair of the Westchester County Republican Party, remains in critical but stable condition at the Donland Center hospital.
>
> Kelly Webster is survived by her mother, Newberry Country Day School trustee, Sandra Webster, and her 13-year-old sister, Danielle. Neither was in the car, but both arrived on the scene.

You could hear the clock ticking. Dani stared at the bank of windows behind Thurber.

Please Help the Blind. Survived by Danielle. Please Help. Survived by . . .

Dani put her hand over her mouth to clamp down on the heaves. "Saraya was vanquished! But Yuras survives. Yuras lives."

No one knew where to look.

Finally, Jared spat. "I don't believe it! Hell, you mean your sister's been dead all this time. This saint of yours . . . well, lick my . . ."

"Thank-you for that icebreaker, Jared. Now, sit down and shut up." Thurber didn't take his eyes off Dani.

She stared at her window.

Please Help the Blind.

Thurber got up and went to her. He clamped his hands over hers and held them. "What happened, Dani?"

"Survived by . . . survived. Jesus God!" The lights, the flashing lights. Not from taking her to the hospital to get her stomach pumped but from that night. Her mother's cell phone had rung. They raced there. "All those lights. The police cruisers, the ambulance, the fire engines. They were flashing, flashing, red, white, red. Mother and I stood there. They wouldn't let us . . . not even her. We had to follow the flashing lights as they took them away, took Kelly away all broken like that. Just took her away."

"Danielle."

"I never saw her again."

Tears washed her face. No one had ever seen her cry. In a place, a room devoted to tears, Dani had never shed one. "It's okay, Dani." Thurber pulled at her with every word. "We'll take care of you. You're safe, you are safe here. I need you to go through it now, Dani. What happened that day?"

The words tugged and then cut loose from her. "I didn't go. I never intended to go. It was all a lie." She withdrew from him. "Evil walks, evil always survives. Never, see? I was sick and tired of it all. The Game, Kelly, always Kelly. She needed so much. She was always, always with me, needing . . . and that stupid, stupid Game."

The dead, flat voice was gone, replaced by a strangled anguish that scratched everyone who could hear.

"But I said I'd do the Game that day because she was just so freaked out by the recital and . . ."

Dani glanced at Kevin, who was gripping the arms of his chair so hard it looked as if his knuckles were going to pop out.

"And I knew I wasn't going to go to the recital. I knew all along. I just went to the ravine to shut her up. To feel less," Dani dropped on her knees and began to rock, "less bad."

Kevin got up and sat down on the floor by her and Scratch. "Why didn't you want to go?" he asked. "You were afraid, right? Afraid that it would all happen again, that he'd beat the crap out of you. That it would be like your recital."

Jared sneered. "So the almighty protector was just a gutless little turd?"

Kevin started after Jared and was yanked back by Scratch. "Chill out," she snapped. "None of you doorknobs knows what real fear is."

"I do," said Dani hugging herself. "I do. It wasn't fear. Oh God, see, that would almost be okay. It was because . . . I'm bad. I deserved to . . . to be hurt." She clutched her shirt collar. "Just bad. But I was good that one time. That time when I was eleven. You should have seen, I was good and pure and Daddy stood up. He clapped for me in the dark. For me! He loved me then because I was so good. He called out, 'That's *my* baby.' Me. For me! *My* daddy. Daddy." She shut her eyes. "I couldn't, I would not watch him get up and clap for her."

Dani swiped at her face and looked at Thurber. "She couldn't be his baby. Not while I hadn't really given up, not really, even then. I was still trying. I thought . . . I would have rather seen her . . . dead."

Kevin inhaled through his teeth.

"I ate a bar of soap," Dani's voice assumed a clinical tone. "I read somewhere that that's what draft dodgers did. I threw up nonstop. There was no question of me going. My mother had to stay with me." She shook her head. "I don't get it. She was a klutz, but on the piano . . . Kelly had genuine talent. Fourth? Just fourth. Something must've happened. She probably got all freaked out that I wasn't there, see? Fourth? She should have got the gold. . . . I could hear it in practice." She shook her head, stunned. "Did he hit her and didn't see? Or was he drunk and didn't see? Or . . . or maybe he went to grab her by the hair and didn't see. It should have been my hair because it always was my hair." She seemed to smile. "I was the protector. I was bad, but at least I was the protector. It was the one true thing I did."

Hard, keening sobs jerked out of her. It was the kind of crying that everyone recognized and pretended not to.

"I promised. I promised. It was supposed to me."

"No!" Thurber clapped his hands. Dani started. "It was not your job to protect. That was wrong, Dani. You were a child, a child who needed protection. It was not yours to give! Do you hear me? Not yours . . . and Dani, you don't know that any of that happened. That kid, the kid in the Suburban, came out of nowhere. It was him that was drunk, not your . . ."

She was oblivious. She shot to her feet. *"Kelly!* Kelly, I'm sorry. I'm so sorry. Dear God, Kelly, please, please forgive me."

Kevin started for her, but was held back by Scratch. Thurber nodded at them.

"Sorry, sorry . . ." Her voice echoed and reverberated all around her. "Forgive me." It was her voice, but they were not her words. Dani had heard those words before. God, her mother's words pleading, begging. "Darling, I'm sorry. I'm so sorry, can you try to forgive me?" But it was Yuras who answered for her. *Forgive you? Forgive you! You were supposed to protect me. How* dare *you ask.*

"Oh-God-Kelly, sorry."

It was wrenching to listen to her. It was wrenching listening to herself. She sounded like an animal. It was as if she didn't know how to cry and was going about it all wrong. A part of her heard Thurber carefully dismiss everyone. They were reluctant to leave. This was too good, too unbelievable. Thurber had to shoo them out one by one.

Dani was crying out of her mind. Only a small part of her was aware that Alison was sobbing and rocking with her. They clung to each other like their lives depended on it.

William Thurber shut the door, returned to his chair and waited.

June 3

Scratch was at her post outside the infirmary corridor, muttering to herself. "Come on, Dani girl." Her shoulders tightened, arching back painfully. "Enough already. Time's a wasting, kid. Remember, we got plans. Snap out of it, Dani." She clenched and unclenched her fists. "Can you die from crying?"

Whenever she could get away, Scratch returned to the infirmary hall to pace, monitor Dani's traffic, check her watch, and sigh for emphasis. Kevin was scooted away as soon as he was spotted, but everyone pretty much let her be. Although she commiserated with Kevin every time he was given the heave ho, she thought that this was actually as it should be. Well, not actually . . . actually she should be in the room with Dani, telling her to stop crying because it was tearing her apart, for Chrissake.

Just then Yolanda swung open the door and Scratch caught sight of Mrs. Webster curled up in an armchair in the far corner of the room. Seeing Mrs. Webster in the shadows both calmed and enraged her. Dani's strangled sobs could be heard through the quickly closing doors. "Je-e-e-sus, Yo," said Scratch. "No scrawny little body can have that many tears in it. You guys have got to stop replacing her fluids."

Yolanda sighed. "Stop going back and forth like that, girl. You're making me dizzy." She grabbed Scratch and put her arm around her. "There. I heard about you hugging Dani. I thought they was having me on, but here we be in a slam dunk of human contact. This is a place of miracles. I say it all the time, don't I, girl?"

"Yup, there's no turning back. I've turned into a Beanie Baby." Scratch rested her head on Yolanda's ample shoulder. "You'll have to lock up your children and pets."

"The world will be a better place for it, girl."

Scratch was so soothed by Yolanda's warmth and lullaby voice that she almost forgot to be enraged. "Oh no, you don't." She extricated herself from Yolanda. "What is *she* doing in there? I've been cooling my butt out here waiting all this time while she—"

"Sh-h-h-h." Yolanda raised a finger to her mouth. "They called the mother last night, and Dr. Thurber said it would be okay if she stayed so long as she doesn't interfere in any way. I don't think she's gone to the bathroom since she got here, poor thing."

"Poor thing, my . . . never mind," sniffed Scratch. "Yolanda, shouldn't you do something about the crying? I mean, even for someone that's nuts, this is nuts, if you know what I mean. Dope her up or dope her down. I can't stand it."

"No, girl." She put her arm around Scratch again.

Again, Scratch didn't resist. She wanted just to curl up and go to sleep in Yolanda's pillowy arms.

"No, girl. Not now. It wouldn't be right. She wants to cry."

"Not like that she doesn't! I know her. Nobody cries like that and for so long." She shook her head. "It can't be right." Scratch resumed pacing. "Make her eat. I have found in dozens of controlled experiments that it is virtually impossible to sob your guts out and eat, say, spaghetti marinara at the same time. Yup, spaghetti would be good."

"Calm down, Alison. You'll wear a groove in the granite." Yolanda folded her arms. "Mrs. Webster has not seen that child cry since she was in kindergarten, girl. Maybe four years old. Think about it. All those beatings, all that shame and hurt for all those years, and she didn't cry. She didn't cry when she heard her little sister was killed. She didn't shed a tear at the funeral. Alison, baby girl, that child has got a lifetime of crying to catch up on. Leave her be."

A crispy keen nurse's aide shuffled over carrying a fresh pitcher of water. She was so startled by the wailing that greeted her when she pushed open the door that she spilt half the pitcher.

Scratch slumped against the wall. "I screwed up, Yo," she whispered. "In Little Group. I was playing God because, well . . . because, that's what I do, you know, and I thought it was a good idea at the time and . . . look, Yo . . . look, what happened. Even Kevin . . ."

"Kevin is a mensch," said Yolanda.

Scratch made a face. "Well, I suppose, but only if you admit that I'm one hell of a woman who happens to have made a big mis—"

Yolanda chuckled, shaking her head. "What an ego, child. It's the curse and salvation of you. Listen to me, girl. Have I ever steered you wrong?"

"Well . . ."

"Listen, I said. Nothing, but nothing, goes on in Little Group without the doctor's fine hand being in on it. He let it happen. It was time." She glanced over to the room and looked immeasurably sad. "You did good. You did good, Alison Mackenzie, because you are good." She shook her head. "You are *good.* Now you're just going to have to find a way to live with that."

"Yeah, but how?" she blinked, a little surprised at herself.

"And nothing goes on in this place of miracles that I don't know about. You hear me?"

Scratch looked away.

"Do you hear me, girl?" She gently cupped Scratch's face in her hand and turned it back toward her. "I know you hear me, child. We understood each other from the first day they brought you here spitting and hollering."

"Maybe."

Yolanda nudged her. "Did we or did we not understand each other from the get go?"

"Hey, one of the ways I can prove that I am a genius is that on day one I 'got' you. I knew right away, that this place, that you, were different. The hacking, my little numbers, whatever. I got that you knew. And I knew that you knew that I knew." She looked up at Yolanda and smiled. "And we were both cool with that."

Yolanda laughed. Her smile heated up the corridor. "But we must swear that we will only use our powers for good, never for evil."

“Of course, only for good,” Scratch nodded gravely. “You’re an amazing first-class human, Yolanda Brigswater, and don’t let anyone tell you any different. I need you to know how much I, well . . .”

“I know.” Yolanda spun Scratch around. “There is not a thing I don’t know, child. Go on with you. Now git, good-bye.”

“Well, okay, but . . .”

“Just git.” She gave Scratch a gentle pat on the butt.

“Dani has to do what Dani is doing. Her Ma is there. It’s all the way it should be, child. All of it. Trust me now. You go.”

Scratch strutted down the hall in her sassiest stride, baggy sweats and all. “You go, girl!” Yolanda called out loud and clear, then more softly, “Go with God.”

June 4

The infirmary was one of the renegade rooms that had missed every single renovation effort inflicted on the rest of the clinic. It was the only honest holdover from the clinic's glory days as a private boys college. Three single beds stood at attention, waiting. Dani occupied the fourth bed. The walls were covered in some lunatic's idea of a cheerful and refreshing print. Birds of every size and description perched on an alarming assortment of twigs and branches, and the whole lot was pinned against bright yellow stripes. There were bald spots around each bed that had been peeled back and written over by bored tonsillectomy patients. *Old man Wilton sucks the big one—E.J. 1957*, etc., etc. The birds reminded Dani of Kelly and made her cry. So did all the twigs and branches. So did the graffiti. Come to think of it, she couldn't draw a breath without thinking of Kelly. Except for fitful snatches of unconsciousness, Dani had been crying for almost two solid days.

Somewhere in all of this, she had actually fallen asleep. When she awoke it was with all the heart-constricting panic of not knowing where you are or why you are.

"Kelly!?"

It was dusk. Not quite dark enough for lights, but not quite light enough to see.

"It's me, darling." Mrs. Webster jackknifed out of the chair. As she did she knocked over a bed tray, sending it clamoring as she stumbled to Dani's side. "Oops."

"Mother?" Dani was almost more amused than she was confused. "Hey, wow. I can finally see that Kelly came by being a klutz honestly."

Her mother retrieved the steel tray. "Yes, well, I am usually much more conscious of being a potential klutz and I have my klutz guard up."

Dani rubbed her eyes, shocked to find them dry. When did she stop crying? "Hmmm. That was close to being sort of funny, Mother."

"Well, then, it's been worth it."

"Huh?"

"Sorry, sweetie. What I mean is that in between visits here, getting my decorator's license, visits to my therapist and support group, and the lawyers—oh, let's not forget the lawyers—I decided to take Developing A Sense of Humor 101." She clutched the lunch tray to her chest as if it were a teddy bear. "You were always funny. Even as a little baby, you had this big, deep laugh, and you would laugh at the most ordinary little things. I thought it might help me . . . us . . . if I could figure out how to light myself up."

"That's lighten up."

"Yes, of course. That's what I meant to say."

Dani snorted at the Kellyism. "Mom?"

"Yes, darling?"

"I'm hungry."

"Of course!" Her mother dropped the tray again and had to retrieve it from under the bed. "Great. I'll go and use this." She brandished the tray like a weapon. "Hungry is good. I'm going to the cafeteria right now. Soup? Yes, soup. When you were little, it was mushroom soup and fries after a fever. But it was pizza when you were upset. We'd order it when . . . no. The most important thing! How could I forget, the most important thing was Jell-O with the real fake whipped cream. Only an edible oil product will do!"

She started to tear out of the room.

"Mother!"

She dashed right back to Dani's bed. "I'm doing it again. Sorry, darling. What would you like, dear? If they don't have it here I'm sure Dr. Thurber will let me go out and . . ."

"Mom!" Dani raised her hand. "We'll just press the button for a nurse's aide. I'm pretty sure that the infirmary is one of those room-service type deals."

"Oh." Her mother looked disappointed. "Of course. That makes sense. Is there anything I could do . . . get . . . anything?"

"I want to see Scratch now."

Her mother began plumping Dani's pillows. "You can't, darling." Pound, pound, pound. "I'm so sorry darling, she's"—pound, pound—"gone. Last night, her and Kevin." Pound, pound, pound. "Oh Dani, darling . . ."

Dani's eyes threatened to well up, but didn't. "It's okay. I knew it was coming. What happened?"

"You did? How . . . never mind. I'm not entirely sure about what happened last night." She sat on the corner of Dani's bed. "That Yolanda, what a remarkable women she is, don't you think? At first, I must admit, she intimidated me a bit. Well, I wasn't sure what to think, but for quite some time now I have realized what an extraordinary—"

"Mother!"

"Oh, I'm doing it again. So they went missing yesterday. The police have been crawling through here ever since. They wanted to come in here, but that Harold fellow put the fear of God into them. Your roommate's stepfather is threatening to sue the pants off the clinic. I think we should press your father into service on this one."

Dani sat up.

"I'm kidding! It was a joke. I'm not getting the hang of this humor thing, am I? Darn, darn."

Dani shook her head. "Maybe you've got to give it a bit of time."

"Yes, time. I hope there's time." She reached over and brushed Dani's hair with her fingertips. "Where was I? Oh yes, then, the boy's parents. Kevin? Well, I heard them! Common," she sniffed. "Let me tell you, I'm rooting for the boy on this one. They're threatening to sue everyone in sight, too. But Ms. Brigswater told me they both seemed inordinately pleased when they heard that he had actually run off with a girl. Can you imagine?"

"Ha!" Dani hooted just as Harold stomped in.

"Yous two want to go blind," he barked as he hit the lights, "or are ya trying to have a seance? Hey, Danno. You stopped sobbing. That's nice, and you're having a chat with your old lady in the dark even without the big kahuna around."

Dani and her mother blinked at each other like a couple of owls. Her mother reached for Dani's hand. Dani didn't pull away. Her mother's hands were rough and torn up. No French manicure, no jewelry, no ring even. Her mother always had such beautiful hands, such beautiful everything, and all of a sudden she just looked like somebody's mom.

"I'm hungry, Harold."

"Well, that's where I come in, you little brat." He winked at Mrs. Webster. "So you got your pick, kid. The cafeteria just opened. Stay away from the hamburger, though. It looks like horse droppings tonight."

Dani kept sneaking peeks at her mother. She looked kind of frayed all over. Right then she was staring out the window, maybe pretending that she was somewhere else, that they were somewhere else. It blew her away.

"Well, Harold, do you think you could find me some mushroom soup, fries, a cheese pizza?"

Her mother turned back to her.

"And, most important, Harold, could we have some Jell-O with real fake whipped cream?"

"It's your funeral, kid," he shrugged. "Besides, you need the calorie count. Yolanda's threatening to stick you in with the lettuce eaters now that your roomy is AWOL."

"Harold?"

"Yeah, brat?"

"Could you make that two Jell-O's with real fake whipped cream?" She squeezed her mom's hand. "My treat."

June 5

The worst part was going back to their room, her room. In a way, it looked exactly like before. Someone had made her bed, but the same pile of clothes in the corner stared at her accusingly. Scratch's half was just as pristine and surgical as ever. But it was empty now. No soaps, lotions, potions, or powders multiplied on the window ledges or tabletops. Her stomach lurched when she caught sight of their dresser . . . just her key chains all by themselves. Dani rummaged through the laundry, rifling through tops, shorts, and underwear until she came across Kevin's beautiful white on white patterned shirt. Holding it tight against her body, Dani settled herself on top of the clothes. She caressed the sleeves. "I'm still here, guys. Don't forget me."

Later that day she met her new roommate, Shaniqua. Standard issue angry, foul-mouthed but gorgeous. Dani was transfixed.

"Don't tell me," Shaniqua snarled. "You ain't never been up close and personal to a black chick before."

"Uh . . ."

"Well, I don't do any dumb white-ass questions on culture,

including hip hop and hair. Got it?"

"Get it."

"Good."

Some things never change. The fire, the pose . . . Dani could smell the fear rising off Shaniqua. Was it that way for Scratch when she first came in? Was it that obvious? Scratch had pushed through over and over again. Torn down the walls. Why? If Dani were a decent person . . . a fully formed human being . . . a woman of compassion . . . There was a knock at the door.

"Get the door, bitch. It's that Uncle Tom, Yolanda."

Dani decided she was comfortable with not being a woman of compassion after all.

Yolanda strode in with the weekly schedule of classes and sessions for each of them. "Good afternoon, ladies. Don't let the paper fool you. I'm here on a body count. Dani, honey, do something about that laundry. The folk will think you're still too nuts to leave. Shaniqua," she leveled her gaze at the girl, "here's your life for this week."

Shaniqua tried to stare Yolanda down, but lost in a heartbeat. She averted her eyes when she grabbed for the schedule.

"Dani?" Yolanda kept tracking her new charge.

"It's cool," said Dani. "I'll give her the grand tour before Little Group at four." While Shaniqua was forming an appropriate snarl, Yolanda vanished. Shaniqua snatched her hairbrush and hurled it at the same corner that stored Dani's entire wardrobe pile. Without blinking Dani said, "You would have really liked my old roommate. She didn't much like me being such a pig either."

Day after day, everything was so much the same, but eerily different. It was enough to drive a person crazy. Her release date had finally been scheduled. Just three days away. Dani chafed under the hours. It was like the time they all got to the airport way early and nothing was even open. All the magazine kiosks and restaurants were closed. What to do, what to do. In family therapy, they talked endlessly about outpatient therapy versus connecting to a therapist closer to home.

And she waited for the call.

Eventually, they all agreed that Dani should continue with a Dr. Elizabeth Reinitz whose practice was just a block away from her new school. Dani even met Dr. Reinitz. She was okay—no Thurber—but okay. And still there was no call, no message. Where were they?

The only thing that made the waiting slightly more bearable was that Jared was gone. Janice, still dumber than paint, was inconsolable. The police had uncovered an impressive stash of amphetamines and Ecstasy in his room during the mauling the clinic underwent when Scratch and Kevin went missing. Jared was sent packing to a juvenile detention center, and there was nothing his parents or the board of directors could do about it.

Apparently, Harold had mistakenly directed the detectives to Jared's room rather than Kevin's.

Despite halfhearted attempts by Dani to steer her clear, Shaniqua was in constant trouble over her mouth. Bobbie, missing Kevin something fierce, clung to Dani. They made for a motley mod squad, but Dani ate with them at the Formica table and even introduced them both to the old oak tree. She felt like C Ward's elder statesman, and that wasn't all bad.

Her mother came a lot. They walked aimlessly around the grounds. Mrs. Webster bubbled on about Dani's new room—"How about a bold plaid, darling?"—her new school, their new life. And still there was no call, no message, no nothing.

"And if you hate the school," her mother said, "Daddy would be happy . . . in fact, I'm sure he would prefer to place you with a good private school if—"

"No way. Uh-uh," Dani grunted. "I can't wait to go to a regular school."

Her mother glowed. "That's just what I told him. And don't you worry, I won't go anywhere near the PTA . In fact, I'll stay as far away as you need me to stay."

"Stay away?" said Dani.

"Darling?"

"Stay away?" she repeated. "It just hit me." She turned to her mother. "The whole thing. The PTA . . . school trustee, president of this and that, chairing the music festivals . . . Were you staying close while you were staying away?"

Her mother looked dejected.

"Oh Mom, what a waste."

Mrs. Webster grabbed at a handful of oak leaves. "You make it sound so much more intelligent and thought out than it was." She methodically shredded a leaf. "What a mess I made, what a mess. Oh Dani, how are you ever going to forgive . . ." She caught herself. "Sorry. We don't have to get into that. I just . . . I just pray that you'll give me a chance to be a mom. Your mom. It's all that matters."

Dani could feel herself tense. In her free-floating discomfort, she zeroed in on her mother's coral necklace. She did always wear it. Always. Dani remembered and somehow that made her even more uncomfortable. "Did Daddy . . . well, I know all about the court restraints and all the custody stuff."

Mrs. Webster crooked an eyebrow at her.

"Yeah, well, Scratch has a lot of gifts, not the least of which is that she's a heat-seeking missile when it comes to information. But thing is, did Daddy ever try to get in and, you know, demand to see me?"

"Well, he was warned, darling. His reputation, the firm's. Why his own lawyers . . ."

"I've been here three months, Mother!"

Her mother sagged. "He did try once, darling. I was adamant and Dr. Thurber agreed."

"How about the family therapy deal?" asked Dani.

"No." Her mother held herself. "No. You were not, are not ready. I said no." She shook her head. "Dani, for once the center held. I'm so sorry if . . ."

She stepped toward Dani, and Dani stepped back.

"It's okay." Dani held up her hand to wave away the image of her father small and searching. "Or it will be. We'll figure it out later. Don't look like that. I . . . thanks for being honest."

"Oh Dani, it's hard. I want so much to make it better than it is. I'd do anything, anything, to make it better." Her mother stroked Dani's hair. She didn't pull away. "I hope that we're going to have time to figure it out. Together." She glanced at her watch. "We had better head back."

They had just reached the courtyard when a window shot up

on the second floor. "Hey, hot stuff!" yelled Harold. "Get your buns up here. You got a call."

Her head pounded. "Who is it?"

"That doctor guy. Scratch's friend, you know, the gynecologist."

"Dermatologist."

"Right, I guess he wants to give ya a facial. Get your bony butt up here."

"Hurry," her mother smiled. "I'll wait here."

Dani was hyperventilating by the time she got to the phone. "Dr. Steve? Hi, this is great, do you . . ."

"Hello, Danielle, I trust you're well. Let's not make this too cloak and dagger, but I'm going to turn you over to someone. Don't exclaim or change your tone or anything. You are just continuing to have a nice catch-up conversation with a friend of your friend, right?"

"Yeah . . . I mean, right. Thanks for asking, Dr. Steve. Dr. Steve? Dr. . . ."

"Dani?"

"Ah-h-l . . ."

"Don't say Alison, you little twerp."

"Right."

"Hey, it's great to hear your voice."

"Me too you."

"Yeah. Just listen, okay? Kev and me are with Dr. Steve and it's all cool. Actually, it's going great, Dani. Well, Kevin is pissed that he can't talk to you, but other than that it's great. Hey, we're even going to this freaky alternative school in the city, and it's a gas. Kevin may actually learn something."

Dani was nodding and grinning into the receiver. Harold ambled by, slowly. She tried to stop smiling. "Yes, I'm coping just fine, thanks for asking."

"Good girl. Keep it up. When is your release date?"

Dani's heart was thumping so furiously she was sure that Scratch could hear it over the phone. "As a matter of fact, it's the day after tomorrow." She glanced out the window and caught sight of her mother sitting cross-legged on the stone bench. She was ringed on all sides by the shufflers. She seemed to be completely absorbed by the oak leaf twirling in between her fingers.

"Whoa. We didn't call a minute too soon, but we had to wait for the heat to settle down a bit. Are my folks still threatening to sue Thurber?"

"I believe so, yes."

Scratch snorted into the phone. "That's just for show. I give them another week. Trust me, they're relieved. Kevin's parents are praising the Lord that I've turned him into a macho stud. I think they're waiting for wedding invitations."

Dani was grinning so hard her face hurt. "So, Dr. Steve, how is it going with you?"

"Well, he's trying, poor thing. But let's face it, he's basically a bachelor guy in way over his head. I mean, he's stuck with two runaways fresh out of a loony bin, ya know?" Scratch giggled. "Last week I asked him to get me a razor so I could shave my legs? He got all freaked out. Man, what a scene. I thought it was hooked into the cutting, but as it turns out, he had been totally gearing up for the girl thing. The poor guy had been prepping to give serious advice about my period or birth control. Leg shaving threw him for a real loop."

"I miss her, too," said Dani grinning into the receiver, "every single day."

Her mother was shredding the leaf now. Meticulously tearing along the veins to leave the delicate skeleton exposed. It was something that Kelly used to do. When she was really, really scared.

"Well," Scratch pressed on, "the point is he's trying, bless his bumbling heart and it's good, Dani. Now say something appropriate, you dope."

Harold walked over again and started rummaging around the desk. "My mother is just fine, thank-you. She's here right now."

"Gotcha . . . and Harold is hovering, right?"

"Why yes, that, too, now that you mention it."

"We're ready for you, Dani. We've talked it all through, even that you're only fifteen. He's got a lawyer lined up for you. I don't know who's more nuts, but he's ready to take you in, too, and it's good, Dani. We'll be family. Realer than any real family."

Her mother examined the leaf intensely, flicked it away. She seemed to crumple in on herself like someone had let the air out of her.

"Dani. It's all set, we got to put this ball in motion. Are you ready?"

Her mother buried her face in her hands. Dani's eyes filled up.

"No." Dani exhaled, feeling like she could float out of the window. "No, thank-you. I don't think so, but it was nice of you to ask." She couldn't trust her voice.

"Holy cow pie, Dani, are you going to give it a go with your mom?"

"Uh-hmm, uh . . . see . . ."

"It's okay. Don't go off on another crying jag. You sure about that?"

Dani blotted at fresh tears with her sleeve. "Well, yes, I think I might be."

"Perfect. You sob at the drop of a hat, and I'm hugging anyone who'll stand still long enough. What a success story we are, girl."

"We sure are."

"Dani?"

"Here."

"It's okay. I got to admit she stuck in there for you. Trust me on this. Me and Kev don't have that. You do."

"Yeah, I . . . well, maybe I do after all."

"Don't worry. When things chill out, we'll all get together. Don't freak, Dani . . . this isn't an either–or kind of thing. It's a lifetime kind of thing. The three of us . . . well, plus Dr. Steve and your mom. Hey, there's more of an *us* to always be us. We'll call you at your mom's place. I'm . . . we're real happy for you, Dani."

Her mother hadn't moved. "It was so sweet of you to call, Dr. Steve. Don't worry about me. If I hear anything, I'll let you know."

"You do that, kid. We'll call you at your mom's. Ciao."

At your mom's? At your mom's? Dani wiped her face again and smiled sweetly at Harold. He rewarded her with a goofy grin. "Well, Dr. Steve doesn't know where they are either."

"Imagine that." Harold glanced out the window. "Your old lady's still out there." He frowned. "Uh . . . I'd take off if I was you. She looks a little off her nut."

"Right!" At your mom's, yeah. Dani ran down the corridor taking both flights of stairs two at a time and almost flattened three shufflers in the courtyard. She was flying until she got up behind her mother. Oh man, was it a genetic thing? Her mother was talking to herself! No, worse, she was singing!

'Twas my own heart, dilly dilly, that told me so . . .

"Mom!"

"Dani!" Her mother blanched. "You startled me. I was trying to . . . see, it was a song I used to . . ." She waved at the shufflers. "I didn't think they'd mind. It was a song that . . ."

"I remember, Mom."

"Oh. Dani darling, please." Her mother stood up, opening her arms. "I promise, I promise to stop hounding you about forgiving me. I know I don't deserve to be . . ."

"Mom, listen," Dani was still out of breath. "I honestly don't know about the forgive part."

"Oh." Her arms dropped. She seemed to fight for a smile. "Well, that's what I wanted to say, that I completely . . . understand, totally. How could you, after all, but do you think, that maybe we could still . . ."

"No."

Out of nowhere a hot wind picked up and scattered debris all over the courtyard. The wind licked at them all, disconcerting the shufflers.

"No, Mom, what I mean is . . . I honest to God don't know what to forgive means. I've been racking my brains, and I could pretend, but I . . ." Dani stumbled, tripping over feeling happy and sad at the same time. Exhausted and exhilarated by the running, by the wind, by everything, ". . . but I won't, okay? No more games. No more Game." She smiled. "The thing is, I don't know if I can forgive you, because I don't know if I can *forgive* me. But I really, really want to try. I want to try so much. Okay? Is that okay?"

Her mother looked like she would blow away.

"Is it enough, Mom?" She was shaking.

"Oh dear Jesus, Dani."

Gum wrappers and leaves swirled around them. Sandra Webster scooped up her daughter into a ferocious bone-crushing hug. An airport good-bye kind of hug.

"It's enough, baby. Oh God, Dani, it's more than enough."

Dani couldn't breathe. She could hardly stand. But this time she didn't need to. Her mother held her strong, breathed for her. Dani let herself go melting into her mother's arms, into her scent. She was locked in an embrace cradled against a wild summer wind that was kissed by a whisper of cinnamon.

MATTHEW WILEY

Teresa Toten was born in Zagreb, Croatia, and immigrated to Canada as an infant. After completing her M.A. in Political Economy at the University of Toronto, she married and moved to Montréal, where she wrote and broadcast for Radio Canada International. She also has lived in Ottawa, where she worked as a speechwriter, press secretary and corporate secretary.

A little more than a decade ago, she moved with her family to Toronto and began in earnest the pursuit of an obsession—writing for young adults and teens. Her first novel, *The Onlyhouse,* was a Canadian Library Association Honor Book, a *Quill & Quire* pick for one of its Four Favorite Works of Children's Fiction, and a finalist for the Ruth Schwartz and IODE Violet Downey awards. *The Onlyhouse* also received a Canadian Children's Book Centre Our Choice Award.

Teresa Toten keeps a busy speaking engagement schedule, giving creative writing workshops to school children across Canada and the United States. *The Game* is her second novel.